12/22

REPLAY

SCHOLASTIC INC.
New York Toronto London Auckland Sydney
Mexico City New Delhi Hong Kong Buenos Aires

REPLAY

a new book

by

SHARON CREECH

starring
Leonardo

with

Aunt Angela Aunt Carmella Aunt Maddalena
Aunt Rosaria Contento Cousin Joey
Cousin Tina Grandma Grandpa Melanie
Mom Nunzio Orlando Papa Pietro Ruby
Uncle Carlo Uncle Paolo Uncle Guido

and featuring
Mr. Beeber

ISBN 0-439-85861-5

12 11 10 9 8 7 6 5 4 3 2 1   6 7 8 9 10 11/0

Printed in the U.S.A.   23

First Scholastic printing, February 2006

Typography by Alicia Mikles

For
Amy Berkower
Joanna Cotler
Karen Hesse
and
Karin Leuthy

for their
wise words
good counsel
and friendship

SCENES

Mr. Beeber's Play: *Rumpopo's Porch*

THE CAST

Leo's Family

Leonardo . . . . Sardine and fog boy, 12

Contento . . . . Leo's moody older sister, 15

Pietro . . . . Leo's younger brother,
the athlete, 11

Nunzio . . . . Leo's youngest brother,
the singer, 8

Mom . . . . (Mariana) Frazzled mother

Papa . . . . (Giorgio) Frazzled father

At School

Ruby . . . . Leo's friend; also the donkey

Mr. Beeber . . . . The drama teacher

Melanie . . . . Dreadful girl

Orlando . . . . A boy who always gets the lead

The Relatives

Grandparents . . . . Grandma and Grandpa Navy,
who always wear navy blue

The Aunties . . . . Pouty Angela, perfect
Maddalena, nosy Carmella,
and invisible Rosaria

The Uncles . . . . Peacemaker Guido, quiet Paolo,
and traveling Carlo

The Cousins . . . . Annoying Tina and Joey

REPLAY

The Curtain Opens . . .

Boy Wonder

From his perch in the maple tree, Leo hears a cry of distress, a high-pitched yelping. He scans the neighborhood, and there, midway down the block, he sees the old woman lying on the sidewalk. Leo leaps from the tree and races down the street.

"Call the rescue squad!" he orders a neighbor peering from her window.

Leo reaches the old woman, takes her pulse. It's weak, fading. "Stand back," he tells the gathering neighbors as he works at reviving the woman.

The woman's eyelids flutter. By the time the wail of the rescue squad car is heard, she is breathing normally, color returning to her cheeks.

"You saved her life," the rescue crew tells Leo. "You saved her life!"

"Hey, sardine! Fog boy! What the heck are you doing? Mom is looking all over for you."

Leo blinks and looks around.

"Did you hear me, sardine? You're going to be in big trouble—"

Leo turns. Trouble? Maybe someone needs him. He dashes for home. Maybe he will get there just in time.

What They Call Him

His name is Leonardo, and his friends call him
Leo, but his family calls him *sardine*. This is
because once, several years ago, when the relatives
were over, shouting and laughing and shaking their
fists, Leo got squashed in a corner and cried, and
when they asked him why he was crying, he said,
"I'm just a little sardine, squashed in a tin."

"A sardine?" his brother Pietro said. "A *sardine?*"

And everyone laughed and took up the chant:
"Leo's a sardine! Leo's a sardine!" Leo's youngest
brother, Nunzio, lisps. He calls Leo *thardine*.

It is not a good idea to call yourself a sardine in
a family like Leo's, who will not let you forget it.

When they are not calling him a sardine, they
sometimes call him *fog boy*. "Hey, fog boy!" his
older sister Contento calls. "Earth to fog boy—"

Some of his teachers even call him *fog boy*. "Fog boy! Wake up! Get with the program!"

Once, the drama teacher called him the *dreamer*, adding that it was not a bad thing to be a dreamer, that all the great writers and artists and musicians were dreamers. Leo wished his teacher would tell his family that.

The Attic

It is raining, pouring, the wind beating against the house. Pietro and Nunzio are fighting, Contento is whining, and Leo flees to the attic. The rain pelts the window, seeping in around the edges, dripping in thin streams down the wall. Leo pokes through the dusty boxes, an explorer on the verge of an important discovery.

Leo unearths a box with his father's name, GIORGIO, on it. Inside the box, near the top, he finds a small blue leather-bound book with yellowing pages containing his father's handwriting in small script, brown ink. On the title page: *The Autobiography of Giorgio, Age of Thirteen.* Leo flips to the middle, where he reads these words, "When I am happy, I tap-dance."

Tap-dance? His father? Leo tries to imagine his father so full of happiness that he tap-danced. This is not an easy thing to imagine, as Papa does not seem very happy lately. Leo closes the book, slips it into his pocket, rummages in the box, pushing aside yearbooks and photographs and letters. Near the bottom, wrapped in tissue paper, he discovers a pair of tap shoes, scuffed, wrinkled, and cracked on the sides.

On the bare wooden floor in the dusty attic, Leo taps. *Tappety, tap, scuffle, tappety, tap.* He slides across the floor, whirl, *tappety, tap,* kick.

⸺

Leo is on national television, tapping up a storm. The studio audience has risen to its feet, and they are applauding wildly. The microphone picks up the host's voice: "Have you ever seen anything like it? Have you ever seen so much talent in such a young performer?"

Leo taps like mad, spins, leaps over a chair.

⸺

"What is going *on* up there? Stop that noise! Stop it, you hear me?" Papa bolts up the stairs. "Sounds like stampeding buffalo!"

"It's just me," Leo says. "I was just—"

"What are you *doing*? Where did you get those

shoes?" Papa spies the opened box. "You've been in my things?"

"I was just—"

"Don't you go through my things. Those are *my* things, what little of my own that I have in this zoo-house."

"But were these really yours?" Leo asks. "Did you really tap-dance?"

Papa scowls at the floor. "Take them off. Put them back."

The rain lashes against the window, and the wind rattles the frame as Leo takes off the shoes, rewraps them in the tissue paper, and returns them to the box. His father kicks the box into a corner and stomps downstairs, pulling Leo behind him. Papa doesn't know that Leo has his little blue book in his pocket, and Leo is not about to tell him.

As he descends the steps, Leo hears the crowd noise fading, "*Bravo! Bravo,* Leo!" He pauses on the steps to bow.

"Hey, sardine-o!" Pietro shouts. "Your turn to clean the bathroom!"

Home

Leo, Contento, Pietro, Nunzio, and their mother are in the kitchen, a small room with faded green and white wallpaper. Leo's mother is flinging papers on the floor. "Bills, bills, bills!" she says. Her eyes roam the room.

"Nunzio-bunzio," she says, "what's with the fidgeting? Set the table."

Contento, who is fifteen and the oldest, says, "There's no lettuce. You're expecting me to make a salad without lettuce?"

Mom peers in the refrigerator. "Aye yie yie!"

Thwomp! The noise diverts her attention. "Pietro? You dropped the meatballs? And you're putting them back in the bowl?"

Pietro shrugs. "It was the sardine's fault."

"Was not," Leo says.

"*Stupido, stupido!*" their mother says.

Nunzio, little Nunzio, echoes his mother. *"Thupido, thupido!"*

Mom slaps a wooden spoon on the counter. *Thwack!* "Might as well cart me away to the asylum right now."

It is all noise and confusion, and Leo feels invisible and wants to press the stop button and rewind.

Leo sees Papa coming up the walk, pulling at his tie, yanking it as if it is strangling him.

"Papa's home," Leo announces.

Leo's mother raises her hands toward the ceiling, as if she is beckoning help from above. "Aye yie yie! Clean up this mess. You know how your father hates a mess!"

Papa slogs in through the door, pouchy bags under his eyes, a mustard stain on his shirt. He glances at the meatballs on the floor, the sauce splattered on the stove and countertops. "A man should have to come home to this?" He turns, stomps back outside, slamming the door behind him. *Wham!*

His wife calls after him. "And who makes you so lucky, that you get to leave? Do *I* get to leave? No!"

"You want to leave?" Leo asks.

Mom says, "Yes! Look at you, all of you, a band of noisy goats!"

Goats. Sardine. Fog boy.

➤━

Leo sits at the table in the nook at one end of the kitchen and presses a piece of peeling wallpaper against the wall. The lights have dimmed, and he hears music, a rousing march.

"So how was school today?" his mother asks.

Leo says, "I'm trying out for the school play!"

Contento says, "I'm on the soccer team!"

Pietro says, "I'm on the football team!"

Nunzio says, "I'm in the choir!"

And their mother says, "What amazing children I have been blessed with!" and their father beams down on all of them and says, "*Sí, sí*, amazing children." He turns to Leo. "And you, most especially!" he says. "An actor! Think of it!"

➤━

Pietro elbows Leo. "Hey! Fog boy! Sardine! Wake up! Did you hear me? Pass the meatballs!"

The Genius

Alone in the room Leo shares with his brothers, he opens his father's blue leather-bound book, his *Autobiography, Age of Thirteen*, and stares at the photographs pasted there: one of his father at age two (according to the notation below the picture), sitting on a porch, arms raised high, as if he is reaching for the sky; and one of his father at twelve, in shorts, barefoot, sitting on porch steps, smiling. The boy does not look like his father, but he seems vaguely familiar.

When Leo hears stomping on the stairs, he slides the book under his pillow, pulls a novel from a stack on the floor, and pretends to read. Contento clomps into the room in a rage, kicking his bed.

"Sardine! Where is Pietro?" she fumes. "I am going to kill him! Kill, kill, kill him!"

"Why?"

"A thousand reasons! That little creep."

"But what did he—"

"A thousand things! That donkey!"

"But—"

Contento is steaming. "Is that all you can say? *But? But? But? Why? Why? Why?* And are you *reading* again? Do you *ever* take your nose out of a book? You're going to turn into a little blind mole."

━━

Leo's brothers and sister vaporize into the ether, leaving Leo an only child, a beloved only child, whose parents dote on him.

"You are our *genius!*" his father says. "Look at this," Papa says to Leo's mother. "He's written a whole novel! One thousand pages!"

"I know!" his mother says. "And it's brilliant! The characters are so vivid—"

"And the plot mesmerizing!" his father adds.

The telephone rings. It's the *Today* show.

"Oh, please, Leo, please will you appear on our show tomorrow?"

"Sure," Leo says. "Happy to oblige."

"We'll send a limousine to pick you up. . . ."

━━

Tapping

Where is everyone? Out scurrying around, the way they do: Mom running errands ("Aye yie yie!" she says. "My life is slave and errand girl!"), Contento at soccer practice, Pietro at football practice, Nunzio with the choir, Papa at work.

So here is Leo. Home. Alone. That rarely happens. Alone!

Leo is a spy, an investigator, roaming from room to room, touching things he's not allowed to touch (Papa's cigars, Mom's pearls, Contento's magazines, Pietro's comic books, Nunzio's wooden horses), king of the house, all by himself. In the kitchen, he climbs onto the counter and reaches the top shelf, pulls down the tin of brownies, hidden so no one will eat them. Leo eats twelve.

Round and round the house he goes, up and down the stairs. King!

Up into the attic, pawing through the box with GIORGIO scrawled on the side. Snares the tap shoes.

Tappety, tap! Whirl, leap, bow, slide. What a feeling—full of taps, completely free, able to do anything!

Tryouts

Leo studies the script for the class play, *Rumpopo's Porch*, written by the drama teacher, Mr. Beeber. It's a short play about a poor old man, Rumpopo, living alone in the woods. Rumpopo fears his life is over and no one cares about him, but then two abandoned children arrive, and when Rumpopo tells them stories, the three of them create a magical world with golden palaces and emerald tables. Everything is transformed: the old man, the children, the tumbledown house. Leo *loves* this play.

There are other characters, too: villagers, an old crone, a dog, and even a talking donkey. The people speak in a funny, old-fashioned way. They say "aye," and "kind sir," and other phrases that make Leo laugh. Leo studies the part of Rumpopo, who seems to be the star of the play. Students can try out for roles in the play, or they can choose to be on the set construction team. Leo hopes he will get a role.

On his way to tryouts, Leo is nervous, fidgety, uneasy. He's been in only three plays before, when he was five, eight, and ten. In the first play, he was a tree. His bark fell off. In the second play, he was an angel. His wings fell off. In the third play, he was a bystander, and he had his first and only line: "Is he hurt?" Leo had practiced that line a thousand, thousand times, but when the time came, what he said onstage was, "Is he glurt?"

Glurt? Glurt? It wasn't even a word. People sniggered on the stage and in the audience. *Glurt!* Leo wanted to die, wanted to take back his *glurt* and deliver his line the way he had rehearsed it, but already the play was moving on, and there was nothing to do but witness his terrible *glurt* swirling in the air, and to hear his brothers chant "Glurt, glurt, glurt!" all the way home in the car.

So, there he is at the tryouts for *Rumpopo's Porch,* hoping to read for—and get—the part of Rumpopo. He will say, as Rumpopo, "Aye, my bones ache," and "My life is empty," and then he will tell about the emerald table, and on like that, with such feeling he will say his lines, yes, he will.

◗━

When Leo is asked to read the part of Rumpopo, he does so, flawlessly and with emotion. The room is silent. Mr. Beeber is in awe of his talent.

The cast list is posted, and there is Leo's name next to the part of Rumpopo. A star is born!

The telephone rings. "Leo? Please can you come on *60 Minutes*? We want to do a special about your amazing acting—"

◗━

"Leo? Leo?"

It is two hours into the tryouts, and the director, Mr. Beeber, is tired of keeping everyone in order, tired of hearing students stumble through the script. Wearily, he motions for Leo and six others to do a scene with the old crone and the villagers.

"Leo? Did you hear me? Read the part of the old crone, please."

Leo does not want to be an old crone. He does not even know what an old crone is. But he wants

Mr. Beeber to hear him speak dramatically, and so he reads his one line, "Ah, yes, the wicked children," and he tries to make the word *wicked* sound extremely wicked. Leo hopes that Mr. Beeber will sense that he is *made* for the part of Rumpopo, and that when Mr. Beeber finalizes the cast, he will make this wise choice.

And so, with great hopes, he seeks out the cast list posted outside the drama room the next day. Dreadful Melanie Morton, she of the golden hair and freckled nose, has the part of Lucia, the second-biggest role. Orlando, who played the lead in last year's play, has the part of Rumpopo. Leo reads all the way down the cast list. There at the bottom, he sees his name, next to *old crone.*

The bad news: he is a nobody, an unknown, and an old crone, to boot.

The good news: at least he is not the talking donkey. That part goes to his friend Ruby.

The *really* bad news he learns later: the old crone is an old *woman.*

"Not to worry!" Mr. Beeber tells Leo when he protests that he is a boy and should not have to play the part of an old woman. "In Shakespeare's time, boys played *all* the women's roles."

"This is not Shakespeare's time," Leo mumbles.

"And that's a pity, mm?" Mr. Beeber says.

Practice

Leo needs someone to rehearse with him at home. It is not enough to know the lines; it is also important to know when to say them, so that he will not be blurting (or *glurting*) them out at inappropriate times.

He asks Contento if she will read with him.

CONTENTO: I have too much homework! Go away!

LEO: Pietro?

PIETRO: A play? Yuk!

LEO: Nunzio?

NUNZIO: I have to thave my voithe for choir.

MOM: Scoot, scoot, I'm busy, can't you see?

PAPA: Sardine, your papa is having a headache, very big one.

And so Leo rehearses alone, reading the whole

play, all the lines, and when he comes to his own old crone lines, he steps forward and loads them with extra feeling. He rehearses in the bathroom because all the other rooms are occupied with people doing homework and watching television and ironing and having headaches.

When the telephone rings, Leo tries to block out the noise. When can an actor find time to rehearse in peace?

PIETRO: (*knocking on bathroom door*) Sardine! Open up! I have to go. *Now!*

And five minutes later:

NUNZIO: (*kicking bathroom door*) Old crone, old crone, let me in!

And five minutes later:

CONTENTO: (*beating on door*) Fog boy! What on earth are you *doing* in there? I want to take a bath! *Now!*

When he next sees his father:

PAPA:	Sardine, come here. What's this I hear about you being in a play?
LEO:	Yep.
PAPA:	You didn't want to try out for football, like Pietro?
LEO:	Nope.
PAPA:	And what role do you have in this play?
LEO:	I'm the old crone.
PAPA:	What's that you say?
LEO:	I'm the old crone.
PAPA:	But—that's an old *woman.*
LEO:	I know.
PAPA:	(*raising his hands in dismay*) I give up.

➤●

CONTENTO:	Sardine! Phone for you—
LEO:	(*on phone*) Yes?
VOICE:	Hello, Leo. I'm a talent scout—I was in the audience at rehearsal, and I'd like to sign you up, on the spot, to play the lead in a new film!

CONTENTO: Hey, sardine! Get your lazy self in here and set the table!

LEO: I'm *not* a sardine! Quit calling me that. I'm Leo. *Leo!*

CONTENTO: Whatever, fog boy.

Leaping

After dinner, Leo lies on his bed. The room, with its three beds and two dressers, is in its usual state: blankets and clothing on the floor, towels draped over a chair, a muddy football on the windowsill. Leo is trying to read. He has made his way through three pages of his father's *Autobiography, Age of Thirteen*, but stops when Contento flies into the room in one of her rages.

He has read the part where his father lists all the people in his family—his mother, father, four sisters (Angela, Maddalena, Carmella, and Rosaria) and three brothers (Paolo, Guido, and Carlo.) Leo knows all these aunties and uncles except one: Rosaria. Never heard of Rosaria. Never!

In his father's book, at the top of the first page is CAST LIST. Next to each name, his father has added a note:

Angela	My oldest sister, temperamental
Maddalena	My sister, loud
Carmella	My sister, jealous
Rosaria	My youngest sister, happy

When Contento clomps into the room in search of Pietro, Leo hides the book and zips down the stairs and out onto the front porch. He leaps from the top of the porch to the grass, races across the yard to the maple tree, climbs halfway up, pauses on a good sitting branch, and surveys the territory (his house; the yard; the neighbors' houses, all big and old like his). Then: back down the tree, running alongside the house and sprinting down one side of the backyard, around the mossy bird-bath, and back up alongside his father's vegetable garden. From there: up the pear tree and onto the top of the garage, across the garage roof, leaping down again to the grass, sprinting down the drive-way and back to the porch. *Ta-da!* Leo rests for a few minutes and begins again, the same route.

On each circuit, the challenge is to see something new, something he hasn't noticed before.

Maybe it is a broken bird's egg on one round, a dead mouse on another, a sparkly pebble on the next round. On he zooms, searching for the new thing.

On this day, Leo thinks of Rumpopo's porch, in the play he is rehearsing. When Rumpopo and the children are on his porch and Rumpopo is telling stories, the most wonderful things happen. Out of the air, they create a magnificent palace. In another scene, an emerald feather becomes a glistening emerald table.

>—

Leo leaps from the maple tree onto his horse, laden with golden medallions. Leo is a knight on a quest. Off he goes around the yard, and there in the birdbath, aha! Sparkly stones. A cache of diamonds? Stolen from a fair lady? Up to the mighty fortress to offer his findings to the grateful fair lady.

"Noble Leo," she says, "how can I ever repay you?"

"There is no need for repayment, fair lady."

The fair lady smiles at him and places her hand on his sleeve.

When Leo returns to the porch, having completed his quest, he is reminded of his father, age of twelve, sitting on his porch, barefoot, smiling at the camera. Leo imagines him leaping off his porch and running around *his* house, or gathered there with his invisible (to Leo) sister, Rosaria.

And on Leo's last round, what he sees is not something in the yard, but something in his mind, a memory, of his father running with Leo around the yard. Papa was wearing a yellow shirt and he was barefoot, and he was holding Leo's hand, and they were laughing.

Then and Now

When Mr. Beeber meets with the cast, he says they have to get a sense of their characters. "You have to know them, understand them. Try to imagine," he says, "what they were like when they were young."

The cast looks puzzled when he says this. It's easy for Rumpopo, because in the play you find out what he was like when he was young. You learn that he and his sister used to turn the porch and the woods into their stage, where they created the golden palace and the emerald table. But in the play you don't learn anything about the villagers or the old crone when they were younger. How could you possibly know what they were like then?

"Mr. Beeber, you wrote the play," Orlando says. "Can't you tell us?"

"No."

"Why not?"

"Well, maybe I don't know. Or maybe I want to know what *you* think. An actor has to bring something of himself to the role."

Ruby, who is playing the front—and talking—half of the donkey, says to Leo, "Hmm, what part of myself is a donkey?"

"There might be some clues in their lines," Mr. Beeber says. "Are they fearful? Jealous? Why do you think that is? What might have happened to them that made them that way?"

Ruby leans toward Leo. "Beeber really wants me to imagine what this talking donkey was like when it was little?"

So many other actors are complaining about being unable to figure out what their characters were like when they were little that Mr. Beeber slumps into his chair and says, "Okay then. What about you? What were *you* like when you were younger? Are you exactly like you are now?" He suggests they jot down notes about their younger selves.

Dreadful Melanie Morton is the only one writing. Leo leans over to see what she's written:

1. I was very cute.

2. I was very sweet.

3. I was very smart.

Leo thinks he might gag.

Mr. Beeber, noticing the cast's distress, says, "Wait a minute. Wait. I've got another idea. Maybe it's too hard to recognize the difference in your own selves. Try someone else. Try a brother or sister."

"My brother is a royal pain," Orlando says.

"But was he always like that?" Mr. Beeber asks.

"Yes."

"Always? Even when he was a toddler?"

Orlando starts writing. Everyone else is writing, too.

The person Leo really wants to write about is his father. Leo has his father's very own book about his younger life, so it should be easy to write about him. But as Leo sits there, he realizes that so far, in the *Autobiography, Age of Thirteen,* his father has mainly talked about everyone else in his family. Leo doesn't have a clue as to what his papa was like, except that he liked to tap-dance when he was happy.

Mr. Beeber strolls around the room, observing everyone else busily writing. He stops beside Leo and says, "Leo? Nothing yet?"

"I was going to do my father, but—"

"Ah, fathers. Those are hard. You have brothers, right? Try one of those." As he walks away, he adds, "And when you've told about the younger person, describe him or her now. Do you see any connections?" Mr. Beeber leaves this question floating in the air as he returns to his own writing.

Pietro and Nunzio

Pietro is eleven, a year younger than Leo, and when Pietro was very young, still a toddler, he would not go anywhere without Leo, and always he was holding Leo's hand or crawling into his lap, even though Leo was not much bigger than Pietro was. Pietro wouldn't sleep in his own bed, either. His mother or father would put him to sleep there, but as soon as they left the room, he'd climb out and appear beside Leo.

PIETRO: Leo? Need you.

LEO: You're supposed to be in your own bed, Papa says.

PIETRO: Not.

LEO: Not?

PIETRO: Not. Not doing.

And so Pietro would climb into bed with Leo, and Pietro was like a warm bear cub, and Leo would tell him the story of What We Did Today, and they would fall asleep like that, crowded in the bed, and sometime in the night, Leo would hear his father come in and remove the bear cub, and it would feel lonely there in Leo's bed.

Now Pietro is all arms and legs and rough boy in his helmet and shoulder pads, and all he talks about and dreams about is football. Leo doesn't understand Pietro's love of football, the smashing bodies, like playing war on the field. Pietro wants only to be with boys who like football, wants nothing to do with his sister—that *yukky girl*—or with boys who aren't into sports.

PIETRO:	Girls stink.
LEO:	Girls don't stink.
PIETRO:	Girls are stupid.
LEO:	Girls aren't stupid.

Leo tries to raise the level of conversation.

LEO:	Pietro, listen to this. (*He reads from a highly intelligent novel.*) "High up on the ridge, he could see below fields of golden wheat—"
PIETRO:	Yuk. Stupid.
LEO:	"—and far in the distance, beyond the golden wheat—"
PIETRO:	Barf.

Sometimes at night Leo misses the little Pietro, the one who would say, "Leo. Need you," and he misses Pietro's bear-cub self, and Leo wonders if he, Leo, has changed from a cute cub into something revolting, and he wonders if anyone misses the younger him.

Leo walks part of the way home with Ruby. She's the only one in Leo's class who is shorter than Leo, and she thinks that's why she got the part of the donkey. "I'm probably the only kid who would fit into the costume," she says.

"Who's going to play the back end of the donkey then?"

"I don't know," Ruby says. "Probably some

little squirt Beeber rustles up."

One thing Leo likes about Ruby is that she doesn't act girly. She has supercurly red hair and pale, pale skin and huge blue eyes, and she always smells good, like soap and oranges. She doesn't do that giggle-thing that so many girls do, and she doesn't act moony over guys, and she doesn't have a fit if she gets wet in the rain.

Ruby says, "So who'd you write about for Beeber?"

Leo tells her about Pietro. "But I don't think I did it right. I told about Pietro when he was young and Pietro now, but I couldn't see any connections. It's like he was one kid when he was little, and he's a different kid now."

Ruby says, "Huh."

"So who did you write about?"

"My brother."

"Your brother? You have a brother?"

"Had."

Leo stops. "*Had?* You mean an older brother who moved away?"

"No, a younger brother."

"Younger? Did he—did he—"

"Yes. He died."

Leo feels sick. He feels like such a wimp.

Ruby shakes her head at his pitiful self. "I'll tell you about it sometime," she says. "Not now, okay? But listen, I don't know why I wrote about him. It's just what came out, but then I couldn't finish because there is no now-brother. I could tell about what he was like when he was little, but he never got big."

In his head, Leo sees a little coffin, and he sees Ruby standing over it, and he feels as if he is going to throw up right there on the sidewalk.

Nunzio, the baby of the family, four years younger than Leo, was born with a mass of soft black hair, like a velvety halo all around his head, and the longest, darkest eyelashes, and ebony eyes so dark you felt as if you could fall into them and disappear.

When Nunzio learned to speak, it was with an endearing lisp:

NUNZIO: Thardine? You help me?

LEO: With what, Nunzio-bunzio?

NUNZIO: Tie my thoothe?

LEO: Your thoothe? Your thoothe are untied?
            Come here, let me see, Nunzio-bunzio.

And Nunzio would trail along with Contento and Leo and Pietro, snagging one of their hands or shirts, hanging on, toddling merrily along, humming little songs, *lo de do, lo de do.*

Even now, at eight years old, Nunzio is still the baby, spoiled by all of them, but how can they help it? His lisp seems so much a part of Nunzio that none of his family can bear to correct him, and instead they encourage his babyish language and way of speaking.

NUNZIO: Thardine? Lithen to me. Lithen to thith
            thong.

LEO: You learned a new thong? Okay, go
            ahead.

NUNZIO: (*Sings, in a clear voice, like beautiful church
            bells.*) "There we go, to the thea, thailing
            on the waveth—"

LEO: It's great, Nunzio.

NUNZIO: Lithen! Not done! "A-wave, a-wave, a-
           wave—"

And on Nunzio will go, singing all day long, sometimes beautiful songs, sometimes unintelligible lyrics from popular songs, and at night as Leo goes to sleep, he hears Nunzio humming and singing.

It is easy for Leo to see the connections between Nunzio-then and Nunzio-now. Nunzio is still a happy, singing, lisping kid. But Nunzio is only eight, and Leo hopes he won't change like Pietro did.

Improvising

The maple tree is the only quiet place today, what with everyone running and shouting and zipping and dashing in the house. There is comfort in the smooth, cool feel of the bark and in the sound of the breeze flipping the leaves. Leo is reviewing his lines for *Rumpopo's Porch*.

"Get in character," the drama teacher, Mr. Beeber, said at the last rehearsal. "*Feel* the character. *Be* the character."

So Leo tries to shrivel up, to be an old crone. He thinks of Great-grandma before she died, a million wrinkles, hollow cheeks, watery black eyes. Leo sucks in his cheeks, squints his eyes. He curls his fingers, like Great-grandma's. Hunches his shoulders. Nearly falls off the branch.

The last rehearsal was a disaster. Everyone goofed, even Dreadful Melanie Morton, of the golden hair and freckled nose, playing the part of the abandoned girl, Lucia, who comes to Rumpopo's house with her brother and their dog. Melanie forgot many lines. The rest of the cast stood around waiting for cues that never came as Mr. Beeber pulled at his collar, saying, "No, back up," and "Wait, that wasn't—" and "Stop!" Finally, he said, "You are all going to have to learn to ad-lib, to improvise, if someone forgets his or her lines. You can't just stand around waiting. The audience will be snoring in the aisles."

For the rest of rehearsal, when Melanie forgot a word or a line (which was often), off she went, talking about things that had nothing whatsoever to do with the play. Here is the way one scene was *supposed* to begin:

RUMPOPO: I am going to the porch now.
LUCIA: Will you tell us about the green woods again?

Dreadful Melanie Morton, however, forgot her line and decided to improvise:

RUMPOPO: I am going to the porch now.

LUCIA: (*Long pause. Very, very long pause.*) Good.
             I mean, that's great, you going off to
             the porch and all. Cool. Everyone
             should have a porch. We've got a huge
             porch, a wraparound porch. Do you
             know what that is?

Rehearsal continued like that until everyone
else was so confused that they were making up things
at random, and Mr. Beeber's collar was nearly torn
off his shirt.

On the way home, Ruby says, "Leo, what do
you think of all this improvising stuff?"

"I like it because if you forget your line, you
can still have something to say, but I don't like it
when Melanie goes on and on—"

"—and on and on!"

"Exactly."

"Improvising is just like normal yakking," Ruby
says. "Like right now, I don't have a script. I'm just
improvising. You say something. I say something.
Like that."

"But in the play, if we improvise all over the place, then it won't be the real play, will it? It'll be a mess."

"Sort of like life, you mean?"

Ruby will do this. Leo will be talking with her about any regular old thing, and she will rattle his brains.

"Imagine if we had a script," she says.

"What? You mean like now?"

"Yes. Think how easy life would be."

"Huh."

If you had a script for your life, Leo thinks, you could look ahead to what would come next. You could see what is going to happen to you. You could read all the thousands and millions of words you will say. You will never again have to wonder *What should I say or do?* because it will all be written there for you.

You could know what dumb things you will do. You could find out if you ever will do anything that *isn't* dumb. But then, what if your script was dull, if you never got to do anything exciting? Or what if something awful was going to happen to you?

What if your script was very, very short? You would definitely not want to know *that*.

►═►

It is Delivery of Script Day, when each twelve-year-old is given his Life Script. A gray-haired woman comes to Leo's class with two large red trunks, which contain their scripts. It is a day of high anticipation. Everyone is fidgety. Some are extremely nervous and feel ill; some are giddy, almost delirious with excitement.

As each student's name is called, he moves forward to receive his script. What follows is bedlam. Those who have received short scripts sink to the floor, wailing. Everyone else flips rapidly through his script, shouting out highlights. Some shout in excitement; others moan in disappointment.

"Harvard! I'm going to Harvard!"

"What? An appliance salesman?"

"What? Not a pro basketball player? A *teacher*?"

"A scientist! A *famous* scientist!"

"I'm getting *married*? To *her*?"

"I'm gay?"

"I flunk out of college? *Twice*?"

They then turn to the final pages of their scripts, and a somber, sober hush falls.

"Cancer. I knew it."

"I'm going to *drown?*"

"Peacefully, in my sleep? Oh, that's good."

"A plane crash?"

"A heart attack?"

"One hundred and twenty years old? Wow!"

The teacher dismisses the class because there is no way any more work will be done that day.

><=

Papa's Script

It is hard for Leo to find time to read his father's *Autobiography, Age of Thirteen,* because there is always someone around, and everyone is so nosy. If they discovered what he was reading, they'd be sure to tell his father, who would probably explode. If Papa didn't like Leo looking through his things, how would he feel about Leo looking through his *life*?

Leo finds a chapter where Papa writes about his own father:

> *One time my father took my brothers and me camping. No sisters allowed. We spent one whole evening packing sleeping bags and tents and food, and we left early the next morning, when it was dark outside. The sun came up when we reached the lake, and it looked like we were in a whole new world.*

We spent all morning fixing up our campsite. We gathered wood and built a roaring fire, and we cooked beans and sausages over the fire. My father didn't say much, but I could tell he was happy, out there in the woods with us.

That is all Papa says about the camping trip. Leo wonders why Papa mentioned that his father seemed happy out there in the woods. Was it because he *didn't* seem happy the rest of the time?

Leo remembers a time Papa took Leo and his brothers camping. He rummages through his schoolbooks and finds the drama notebook in which he has written about Pietro and Nunzio. He adds:

One night, Pietro, Nunzio, and I helped Papa pack the car with the tents and fishing poles and food. Contento wanted to come too, but she was sick. In the early morning, Papa woke us, saying we were going on an adventure. "Shh, very quiet, very secret," he said.

We piled into the car, sleepy and groggy, and

rumbled along until we reached the campsite. The mist was rising off the lake, and it looked eerie. By the time we'd set up our tents, the sun had cleared the mist, and the lake was calm and quiet. We jumped in and splashed and swam. Later we fished. I caught two! It was a great day.

That night, Papa told a ghost story, which scared us, so we all slept in one tent. Papa had to tell us a funny story so we wouldn't be scared anymore.

Papa seemed very happy then. He does not seem so happy now.

Obsessed

Leo is obsessed with that strange exercise Mr. Beeber gave the cast, writing about people when they were younger and how they are now. Leo tries to do one about himself but can't do it. He feels as if he's always been the same.

I was always in the middle or on the edge. Watching.

He tries again:

It was like everyone else was in a play and I was the audience. I couldn't see myself, but maybe everybody feels this way. You never see yourself (unless you look in the mirror). You only see everyone else. I still feel that way.

Pretty sad, Leo thinks.

He finds his mother in the kitchen, her head in the cupboard beneath the sink.

"Mom? What was I like when I was little?"

"Look at this mess! Water dripping everywhere! Get me the bucket—"

Leo retrieves a bucket from the basement. "Mom? What was I like when I was little?"

"Isn't there some valve thingy to turn off this water?"

Leo peers under the cupboard. "This one, maybe?" He turns the valve, and the water slows to a drip and then stops.

"Well, at least the water has stopped," she says. "Now what?"

"Maybe Papa can fix it."

Leo's mother sighs. "Sardine-o, the way Papa would try to fix this is by bashing the pipe with a wrench and calling it a lot of nasty names, and then the pipe would break and then—"

"Mom? What was I like when I was little?"

"What? I don't know. You were you."

"But really, what was I *like*? Was I different from now?"

"Hand me that rag. Different? What do you mean, different? Of course you were different. First you were an infant and then a toddler and you had to learn to walk and talk, so of course you were different. Not that rag, the other one."

"But what was I *like*?"

Leo's mother turns to him, a rag in each hand. "You were sweet and curious. Sometimes you said funny things, like once you said, 'Do I look like a potato?'"

"A *potato*?"

"Yes, a potato. Another time you said you were going to make dirt when you grew up."

"Make *dirt*?"

"Yes."

"But why would I say that? You can't *make* dirt."

Leo's mother is pulling things from the cupboard. "What a mess!"

"Did you write all that stuff down, the things I said?" Leo asks.

"No, alas, I did not. I was a *leetle bit busy*, sardine-o."

A potato. A dirt maker. This is not very enlightening to Leo, and because he cannot write about himself, he turns to his drama notebook and writes about Contento.

He remembers following Contento from room to room, and down the sidewalk, and through the park, and she would take his hand and say, "Here, Leo, take my hand, don't fall." This was before he became the sardine and fog boy. She'd say, "Here, Leo, I will show you how," and "Here, Leo, I will read to you." That was a kind and generous Contento, a big sister, full of importance and love.

"Here, Leo," she would say, "kick the ball with me." And even when Leo couldn't kick the ball, or couldn't kick it far or in the right direction, Contento would laugh and whiz past him and rescue the ball and dribble it nimbly with her feet, her cheeks ruddy, her dark hair flying. Leo thought she was amazing and glorious and that she could do anything and everything. Sometimes at night, she'd lean against his bed and talk to him about soccer or her friends, anything at all, chattering on in the dark room to her friend, her brother.

Leo doesn't know when Contento began to change. Maybe it wasn't overnight; maybe it was slower than he imagines.

One day: "Quit following me everywhere, sardine. Are you my shadow?"

Another day: "Don't hold my hand. You're too old for that."

And another day: "Will you *never* learn to kick that ball? What is the *matter* with you?"

And one night: "Go talk to Nunzio and Pietro. I'm too tired."

There were the rages, too, coming out of nowhere. One minute she'd be quietly sitting there, and the next minute she'd be throwing pillows or clothes, shouting at the others to be quiet or go away.

At the dinner table one night, Contento sat there, with her bottom lip curled out, pouting:

PAPA: Pout like that and a big crow will land on your lip and peck your nose.

PIETRO: (*forming his fingers into a pecking bird and
            snapping them in front of* Contento's *face*)
            Peck, peck, peck, peck—
(Contento *bursts into tears and flees the table.*)
PAPA: What? What did we say?
MOM: *Zitti! Zitti!* Quiet, everybody! Leave her
            alone. She's just trying to grow up.

And Leo wondered if that meant that he would
have to turn into a moody, raging boy in order to
grow up.

Today, on the way home from school, Ruby
says, "You know why it's so weird writing about
people when they were younger?"

"No. Why?"

"Because we're kids. We're always thinking
about *now*, about how to get through each day
without being a complete moron, or else we're
thinking about what's ahead, what we're going to
do, what we're going to be."

"Huh," Leo says. He doesn't realize things like
that when he's talking. He only makes sense of

things when he is alone, thinking, or when he writes.

Ruby stops, puts her hands on her hips, and says, "*Old people* think about when they were young."

"Huh."

"And isn't the whole point that you can change? You might be a dorky, little, nobody kid, but you might be an amazing grown-up."

Leo wonders if she means him, personally. Does she think he's a dorky, little, nobody kid? He is about to ask her this when she says, "I don't mean you, Leo. I'm just saying, that's all."

"But do you think you could also be a happy kid and an unhappy adult? Like maybe the old crone was a cute little kid, very happy."

"So what made her into an old crone? Why didn't Beeber put that into the play?"

"I don't know," Leo says. "And why didn't he give the old crone more lines? If I'd written this play, I would have given her lots and lots more lines, and I'd have made her able to become invisible or to read people's minds or to do other astonishing things."

"Well, if *I'd* written this play," Ruby says, "I'd certainly have done something more with that donkey."

The Shoes

Home alone again, silence and space! It is Saturday, and Mom and Papa and Nunzio are out doing errands, Contento is off with her friends, and Pietro is at football practice. Leo assumes no one even noticed that he would be there alone, or he might have been dragged out for errands.

In Papa's *Autobiography, Age of Thirteen*, Leo reads the part where Papa tells about finding the tap shoes:

> *The tap shoes, like new, were sitting on top of an open trash can. An old man was sitting on the porch. I asked him if he was throwing away these shoes.*
>
> *"Take them, take them," he said. "No good to us."*

I tried them on. A perfect fit! The old man smiled at me. I tapped all the way home.

Rosaria wanted to try on the shoes. They were, of course, too big, but she put on three extra pairs of socks and then she tapped all around the room, around and around and around.

When I am happy, I tap-dance.

Leo darts up to the attic, puts on the shoes, and off he goes, tapping, round and round the attic, and as he taps, he practices his old crone lines:

OLD CRONE: I will find out (*tappety, tap*) what that old Rumpopo (*tappety, tap*) is up to (*tappety, tap, leap*).

Leo is in a play on Broadway, rehearsing the part of a young, poor boy who dances his way to stardom. The other actors stand in the wings during Leo's scene.

"You ever see anybody tap like that boy?"

"Never saw anything like that in my life!"

As he finishes his scene, there is a clamor at the

stage door. Teenage girls are screaming for Leo.

"Leo! Leo! Leo!"

Leo wipes the sweat from his brow and goes to meet his fans.

A door slams. Commotion below. "Sardine! You up there? Your turn to take out the trash!"

As Leo returns the tap shoes to the box, he wonders if, like his father, he tap-dances when he's happy, or if it's the tapping that *makes* him happy.

The Relatives

L eo's family and some of the aunties, uncles, and cousins from his father's side of the family, and his father's parents, Grandma and Grandpa Navy (that's not their real name; it's what Leo calls them because they always wear navy blue clothes) gather for Sunday dinner at Leo's house.

On the front porch, Auntie Angela is bristly and sour. "I'm not going in," she says.

Uncle Guido, the peacemaker, says, "Oh, come on, Angela—"

"I do not want to see Maddalena and her perfect children."

In the front hallway, Auntie Maddalena says, "Angela is being a pain."

Leo's mother, Mariana, says, "Oh, Maddalena, don't be silly."

"Don't call me silly."

Leo wanders to the back porch, where he overhears his cousins, Tina and Joey.

Tina says, "Nunzio still has his stupid lisp."

Joey says, "What a baby."

"And Contento's hair—did you see that?"

"Looks like a monster wig."

"And the sardine—you'd think he slept in those clothes!"

"For two weeks!"

Leo glances at his clothes. They look okay to *him*. He slips back into the kitchen, where Grandma Navy is complaining to Auntie Carmella.

"Didn't Mariana make potatoes? How could she not make potatoes?"

Auntie Carmella, who loves to hear Grandma Navy complain about Leo's mother, says, "I *told* you we should have dinner at my house. I *always* make potatoes."

Grandma says, "Where's your brother Carlo?"

Auntie Carmella shrugs. "Traveling. As usual."

"He travels too much. Where's that husband of yours?"

"Golfing. As usual."

"He golfs too much. And where are my grand-children? You'd think they would be at the door to welcome their grandmother."

She spots Leo as he is about to duck back out of the kitchen. "You there," she says.

He's caught. "Hi, Grandma."

She says, "Pietro—"

"I'm Leo."

"Pietro, Leo, ack! So sometimes I mix you up. I have so many grandchildren!"

Leo makes an excuse, says that he's looking for Papa, and he makes his way to the garage.

Grandpa Navy and Papa are there.

Grandpa says, "You got a new car?" The way he says it, it sounds like, "Are you *nuts*, getting a new car?"

Papa says, "Not completely new. It's used. Four years old."

Grandpa taps the fender. "I've had my car for twelve years. If you take care of them, they last forever."

Papa closes his eyes. He is trying to stay calm.

Grandpa sees Leo. "Well, who's this? Pietro?"

"I'm Leo. I'm the short one."

"You still playing football?"

"That's Pietro. I'm an actor."

Grandpa snorts. "Actor? Don't be silly. What kind of thing is that to be? Be a doctor. There's always a need for doctors."

As everyone sits down to dinner, Papa says, "I'd like to propose a toast—"

Grandpa interrupts. "*Mangia, mangia!* Let's just eat. I'm hungry."

Mom says, "Where's Angela?"

Auntie Maddalena says, "On the porch. Pouting. As usual."

Uncle Paolo sits quietly, smiling absently at everyone. He doesn't need to talk because Maddalena will speak for him. Occasionally, he begins a sentence, but he does not need to finish it.

"Is Carlo—"

Maddalena continues for him. "—traveling again? *Again?*"

Over at the kids' table, cousin Tina says, "Mom! Mom! Pietro hit me."

Pietro says, "You big baby."

Cousin Joey pinches Nunzio and calls him a little booger.

Nunzio says, "Thtop it."

Auntie Carmella points her fork at Leo's mother. "Mariana, you really should do something about Nunzio's lisp. You need to send him to a speech therapist."

Leo's mom chews her food, says nothing.

Back at the kids' table, cousin Tina says, "Hey, fog boy, I hear you're going to be an old witch in a play."

Leo is thinking that he'd like to dump the butter in her lap. "It's old crone, not witch," Leo says, "and it's a very important part."

Cousin Joey chants, "Old crone, old crone, the sardine's an old crone!"

Over at the big table, Grandma Navy says, "Why can't he play an old man? Why does he have to play an old woman?"

Grandpa says, "Where're the potatoes?"

Leo says, "Hey, Grandma—"

She says, "Hay is for horses."

Leo tries again. "Grandma, who is Rosaria?"

Papa gasps. "Leo!"

Auntie Maddalena gasps. "Leo!"

Grandma Navy rushes off to the bathroom, saying, "Oh, oh, oh."

Papa ushers Leo to the kitchen. He says, "Where on earth did you—why on earth—how did you—why did you ask about Rosaria?"

"I—I—"

"Who told you about Rosaria?"

"I—I—"

"Was it Auntie Angela?"

"I—I—"

"Go back to the table. Do not ever mention Rosaria again, you hear me?"

━●━

As Papa proposes a new toast, the room fills up with blinding light, and the table and the dishes and the glasses all turn into solid gold. Emeralds rain down from the ceiling. Everyone says, "Wow!" except for Tina and Joey, who have been turned into donkeys. They say, "Hee-haw."

━●━

Papa

Leo wakes in the middle of the night, thinking about Papa. He'd been having a dream, and in it, Leo was younger, and he was in the garage, afraid, looking for Papa.

It is dark in Leo's room. He hears Pietro snoring and Nunzio turning in his bed. Leo grabs a flashlight and opens Papa's *Autobiography, Age of Thirteen*.

> *I love to swim. The water is quiet and I feel like a fish. I am weightless and free in the water. Sometimes I dive down, down, and I feel as if I could live in the water, rolling and diving and splashing all day long.*

Leo tries to picture his father rolling and splashing in the water.

When Leo was younger, Papa had thick, curly hair, and he seemed to Leo to be big and strong and handsome, like a movie star. He taught his children how to swim, sometimes took them fishing, and loved to pile them all in the car and go for drives in the country. They would stop at a park and have a picnic, and Papa would throw baseballs and footballs, laughing his deep laugh.

Sometimes on Sunday, Papa would take his children to see old Mrs. Tonnelli, who used to work in his office. Papa would give her vegetables from his garden, or, in the winter, a basket of oranges or apples. Mrs. Tonnelli would let Leo play her piano while she and Papa visited.

Once, Papa took Leo to his office on a Saturday. Papa was an accountant, and normally he did not work on the weekend. Papa let Leo sit in his chair and open his desk drawers, and he let Leo use the stapler and the red and blue pencils on clean white paper, and Leo looked around at the maze of cubicles and desks and thought how terrific it would be to work in a place like this, with your very own desk and stapler and pens and pencils and paper.

And Leo remembers one other thing, too. Each night Papa used to go into his children's rooms and say good night to them, one by one, sitting on the side of each bed, listening to whatever important things they had to tell him, and then he would smile and kiss them, and wish them *bello* dreams, no bad ones allowed.

Three years ago, Papa had a heart attack. Leo had gone out onto the front porch after dinner. He leaped off the porch and climbed the maple tree and jumped down again and raced alongside the house, down one side of the yard, around the birdbath, and there, as he started up alongside the vegetable garden, he saw Papa lying in the dirt, alongside the tomato plants.

Leo froze. He couldn't move, couldn't talk, couldn't think. A crow shrieked from the top of the garage, jolting Leo. He touched his father's leg and then he crawled into the row and touched his father's arm.

"Papa? Papa?"

Papa's eyes were closed, his face ashen. Leo thought he was dead.

He ran to the house, but still he could not speak. He grabbed his mother, pulling her outside.

"Stop that," she said. "What on earth is the matter with you?"

Leo pulled at her arm, still unable to speak.

"This better be important," she said.

Leo and his brothers and sister had to wait at home with Auntie Maddalena while Papa was taken to the hospital, and for the next week, while Papa was being operated on. Leo was sure Papa was going to die, and he and Nunzio and Pietro and Contento all cried and wailed like banshees, completely inconsolable, not wanting ice cream or chocolate cake or any of the things that Auntie Maddalena offered them to take their minds off Papa in the operating room.

Leo hid in the bathroom, wishing he had been able to do something for Papa when he found him in the garden. Leo was unable to imagine his life without his papa in it and felt desperate to fix him, to make everything better, the way it was before.

One evening, Leo found Nunzio curled in a ball on the floor of their room.

LEO: Nunzio? Nunzio-bunzio? Don't cry.
NUNZIO: Papa ith dying.
LEO: No, no, he's not dying. He's not. He's getting an operation. He's getting fixed.
NUNZIO: Dying.
LEO: No, no, you'll see. Soon he'll be home and he'll be fine. That's what Auntie Maddalena says.
NUNZIO: Promith?
LEO: Promith.

But Leo didn't believe what he'd promised, and even when his mother called later that evening to say the operation went well, and that Papa was in recovery and they would be able to see him in a few days, even then Leo knew Papa was going to die before Leo saw him again.

Fortunately, though, his papa did not die, but

he was never the same as the papa that Leo remembered before the heart attack. Papa seemed to move more slowly and tentatively. No more running or jumping or throwing baseballs. He started to lose his hair, little by little, until a round shiny patch replaced the thick curly hair. He no longer liked to take drives in the country, and in the evenings he would rest, and when Leo would go in to say good night to him, sometimes Papa would be sleeping already.

Papa seemed to lose his patience for even the smallest things. He called the can opener a "ratty, useless hunk of metal" as he bashed it on the counter, and he had a regular fight with the side door, kicking it and calling it names ("mumble-mumble rickety piece of tin!") when it stuck.

But every now and then, on the weekend, Leo's father will laugh, and sometimes Leo can hear the old laugh in there, and sometimes if Leo closes his eyes, he imagines it is still the other Papa.

The Bird

Saturday! Huge red and gold leaves are falling, falling, sifting through the air, landing on Leo's head and coating the ground, as if someone has spread a magical carpet all around. In the maple tree, Leo studies the whole neighborhood in all its red and gold, and he hears Nunzio singing in the driveway, *lo de do, lo de do.* He sees Pietro with the neighbors down the block, jumping into piles of leaves.

Leo leaps from the branch, *poof,* and over the rhododendron bush, runs alongside the house and down one side of the backyard, and he is just rounding the birdbath when he sees, barely visible in the leaves, something silvery. It's a spoon, bent. Leo sticks it in his pocket, and as he scrambles up the pear tree and onto the garage roof, he remembers Nunzio digging with the spoon last month.

LEO:	What are you looking for, Nunzio-bunzio?
NUNZIO:	Petie.
LEO:	The parakeet? Is this where Papa buried him?
NUNZIO:	Yeth. I think.
LEO:	And you're digging him up?
NUNZIO:	Yeth.
LEO:	Do you think that's a good idea?
NUNZIO:	Yeth.
LEO:	Why?
NUNZIO:	I want to see if he'th thtill there.
LEO:	Where else would he be?
NUNZIO:	Heaven, of courth.

Leo sat there, watching Nunzio dig with the spoon, not wanting him to find Petie, not wanting him to be alone when he discovered the moldy shoe box with its moldy remains of Petie. Nunzio dug a long time, and at last he said:

NUNZIO:	I gueth he'th gone.
LEO:	Petie? To heaven, you think?

NUNZIO: Yeth.

LEO: You think he took the shoe box with him?

NUNZIO: Yeth.

Nunzio seemed happy and satisfied. The next day, Leo probed in the garden, in a nearby spot. He was sure Nunzio had dug in the wrong place. Leo found nothing. He tried another area. Nothing. He got the shovel from the garage and dug some more.

Papa had brought the bird home one day in a small white cage. This was about a year after his heart attack, and it was an unusual thing for Papa to do. He'd always said pets were too messy, and when they'd once seen parakeets in a pet shop, Papa had said it was a shame, that birds shouldn't be caged, that they should be allowed to be outside, flying free.

So the whole family was surprised when Papa walked in the door, carrying the cage with a blue and white parakeet. Papa tried to look serious, but he kept grinning at the little bird. He said, "Somebody at work couldn't keep it." He shrugged, as if there had been nothing else he could do but take it. "Its name is Petie." Papa bent toward the cage. "Hi there, Petie."

At first, everyone wanted to touch the bird and feed it and talk to it, but soon Mama, Contento, and Pietro lost interest, and it was only Papa and Nunzio and Leo that paid any attention to Petie. Every day when Leo would come home from school, he'd open the cage. Petie would jump onto Leo's outstretched finger and cock his head at him, saying the only word he knew: "Pretty. Pretty. Pretty."

Petie would sit on Leo's shoulder as Leo went up to his room and as he did his homework. Petie hopped onto the desk and sometimes flew a lap around the room. "Pretty. Pretty. Pretty."

At school, when Leo told his friends he had a parakeet, one of them said, "A bird? What can a bird do?" Another said, "A dog is much better than a bird."

One day, Petie stopped talking and tweeting. He'd hop onto Leo's finger, but he wouldn't fly. He didn't look right. A few days later, while Leo was holding him, Petie pressed his tiny head against Leo's chest, as if he were trying to rest there. Leo held him for a long time, stroking his feathers. When Papa came home, he touched Petie, still in Leo's hand, still pressed against his chest.

"Leo?" Papa said.

"I know," Leo said. "I think he died."

When Papa lifted Petie from Leo's hands, there was such a look on his face, troubled and sad. Leo felt so heavy, as if his clothes were made of concrete, and as if the air were too thick to breathe. At night, under his covers, he cried. The next day at school, Leo wanted to tell his friends about Petie, but he couldn't do it. How could you say your bird died? Who would understand what that meant?

Leo was remembering all this as he dug in the garden. He dug and dug and dug. Nothing. Maybe Nunzio was right. Maybe Petie had flown off to heaven, taking his shoe box with him.

The Abysmal Cast

Sometimes the cast is awful. Half the people don't know their lines yet. Hardly anyone has learned cues. Characters enter and exit whenever they remember, which is rarely at the right time, and actors fall out of character as soon as they say their lines: the donkey/Ruby blows her nose, and Lucia/Melanie twirls her hair like a ditz. Melanie, who thinks the whole play revolves around her, stands in front of other characters and coughs or yawns when the old crone or the villagers have lines.

They rehearse the first of the porch scenes, where Rumpopo tells the two abandoned children the story about the feather turning into an emerald table. Everyone is suddenly curious as to how this will happen onstage, and if there will be a real emerald table, and so Mr. Beeber has to stop and explain about the set and lighting and music. "It'll all work, just trust me," he says.

"But will the table be *real*?" Melanie asks.

"Yes, it will be real."

"But how are we supposed to rehearse without the real table?"

"Just imagine," Mr. Beeber says. "Please."

Next, they rehearse a scene between Leo and the donkey.

DONKEY: (*to old crone*) This is an opp-opp-port—this is an upport—this is an—what is this word anyway? Do you really think a donkey would say this?

OLD CRONE: Just say it, Ruby.

Mr. Beeber interrupts: "Stay in character! Stay with the script!"

LUCIA: If there's going to be a real dog in the real play, why don't we use a real donkey?

Mr. Beeber interrupts: "Stop! Stop! This is abysmal! Abysmal!"

━●

Leo leans against the wall and closes his eyes.

Orlando and Melanie get sick. Mr. Beeber selects Leo to play Rumpopo and Ruby to play Lucia. They are brilliant. They also respect the donkey and the old crone because, as Mr. Beeber says, "Every part is important; every line contributes to the whole." Mr. Beeber is so impressed that he announces that Ruby and Leo are being transferred to a special school where they will get to do drama all day long, and they will not be donkeys or crones, either.

━●

"Leo? Leo? You walking home or not?"

"What? Oh, sure, Ruby, sure."

Many Papas

Leo is all confused about Papa. There is not just the papa who was his papa when Leo was little, and the papa who is now, but also the papa-before-he-was-a-papa, the one in his *Autobiography, Age of Thirteen*. For Leo, reading Papa's book is like reading a story about someone else. There is a boy in a big family, who likes to swim and to tap-dance, and he talks fondly of Rosaria, the missing sister.

One chapter makes Leo shudder:

> *One incident that stands out clearly in my mind dates back to when I was seven. My father had an old motorcycle which he kept down in the cellar of our apartment building. Rosaria and I decided to go down and play with it, to pretend we were riding.*
>
> *Another boy in the building, Morris, was*

down there, and he didn't seem to like the idea
that we got to play on the motorcycle. He situated
himself before the furnace and poked the coals.

Suddenly a bright idea came to him. How
about putting the hot poker on somebody's neck?
Sure enough, on somebody's neck he put it. Whose
neck? My neck. I wasn't sure what had happened.
I began to scream. The rest is obvious. I was
taken to the doctor. I was out of school for
twenty-six days.

And from there, Leo's father moves to something else. Leo rereads the hot-poker passage. *The rest was obvious,* Papa says. But it isn't obvious to Leo. How long did Papa scream? What had that felt like, a hot poker on his neck? Was he scared? Did he cry? Was Rosaria scared? What happened to the boy, Morris?

Leo wants to ask his father all these questions, but he doesn't know how to do it without Papa knowing that Leo has been in his things, that he is reading his book. In the garage on the day Leo reads this chapter, he stands behind his father, studying his neck. On the left side are ripples of puckered skin. Scars. Leo had seen this rippled skin before but hadn't thought it was unusual. He hadn't wondered how it got that way.

"Papa? What's that on your neck?"

His father's hand brushes at his skin. "What? Is there grease on there?"

"No, that—that scar."

His father dumps a tin of screws onto the work-table. "Oh that," he says. "It's nothing. Why can't a person find the right screw when he needs it? Look at this mess."

"But how did you get it, that scar?"

Papa shrugs. "I got burned. When I was little. Sardine, go ask your mother if there are any more screws in the house. Stupid screws."

So, there is this whole other person who is Leo's father, before he was Leo's father, and Leo doesn't know him, except for what he reads in his book. When he finishes Papa's book, will he know all about this other person? Leo doesn't think so, because Papa does not tell if he cried, if he hurt.

But then, maybe the fact that he does *not* say that he cried or hurt says a lot about him.

At night Papa used to gather Leo and Contento and Pietro on his lap (this was before Nunzio was born), and he would tell them the story of What We Did Today, and somehow he made whatever they had done seem exciting and adventurous. If they'd only walked to the corner store, he'd make it seem as if they had been on an adventure.

"We crept down the sidewalk," he'd say, "in the early morning. We were on a mission: to find the miracle bread! Someone was following us . . ." and on he would go, like that, spinning the story for them.

Once, when Nunzio was a baby and was sick with a fever, and crying, Leo took a turn rocking him. Leo sang to Nunzio a while, and then he told him the story of What We Did Today. Leo can no longer remember the exact story he told, but it was something about a baby whose crying turned into singing, such beautiful singing that everyone said,

"More, more, baby! More of that sound!"

Leo's papa stood in the doorway, gazing down at him. "Leo, you make gold from pebbles," and the way he said it, Leo could tell that this was a good thing, though he did not know exactly what Papa meant. It seemed to Leo that he—Leo—was only doing what Papa did every day, taking little moments and dressing them up so that they were more pleasing to your eye, your ear, your mind. And once you had dressed them up like that, they took root in your mind, replacing the other, more drab or hurtful ones.

Walking home with Ruby, Leo asks if her parents seem the same now as they did when she was little.

She doesn't hesitate. "No way!" she says.

"They were happier then—when you were little?"

"Sure."

"What do you mean, 'sure'?"

Ruby stares straight ahead. "I mean, of course they were happier then. That's when everything was fine. That was before my brother got sick."

"Oh. Sorry."

"Were *your* parents happier when you were younger?" she asks.

"Yeah."

"So did something happen? Something that changed everything?"

Leo stops. "I was going to say that us kids got older, and we weren't so cute anymore, and we were probably a pain, but—"

"What?"

"Things started to change when my father had his heart attack."

"He had a heart attack? That's a big thing, Leo. He probably got scared. He's probably afraid."

"My father? Afraid?"

"Yeah. It's possible."

"Huh."

Leo had always thought being a grown-up was the greatest thing in the world. All that freedom to do whatever you want! You don't have a bunch of teachers telling you what to do, and you don't have to follow everyone else's rules, and you can stay up late and eat as many doughnuts as you want, and you can be whatever you want. Why would his papa be afraid or unhappy when he has all that freedom? And if you have all that freedom to do whatever you want, then why isn't everyone a brilliant scientist or a rock star or a millionaire or a beach bum?

Leo wonders if his father regrets being a father.

Goals

Leo is not home alone. *Everyone* is home, taking up all the spaces. Leo snares his father's *Autobiography, Age of Thirteen*, along with his coat and hat and gloves and an old blanket, and now he is on top of the garage. Two squirrels skitter up the pear tree and leap onto the roof. Seeing Leo, they freeze and then flip their tails at him and scamper back down the tree.

Leo reads the chapter titled "Interests," in which his father says:

> *I like baseball (batting especially) and gymnastics because I feel strong when I do these sports. When I'm not doing sports, I sometimes write poems (but I would not admit it to very many people) and I like to sing, especially with Rosaria and sometimes at church.*

Huh? Leo thinks. *This is my father? Poems? Singing? Church? Who is this person?*

At the end of the chapter, Papa makes a list of his goals, in two categories. The first one is:

A. High School
    1. To be on the honor roll.
    2. To be captain of the gymnastics team.
    3. To write for the school paper or the yearbook.
    4. To be in the choir.

Beside each of those numbers is a check mark in blue ink. It looks to Leo as if these marks were added later, so he assumes that his papa accomplished each of these goals. The check marks are solid and bold, as if he is proud of these achievements.

The second category follows:

B. Life
    1. To be a singer.
    2. To be a dancer.
    3. To be a writer.
    4. To be an athlete.

This is all news to Leo. There are no check marks next to any of these. Leo notices that "to be a father" or "to be an accountant" is not on Papa's list. This bothers Leo, and so, there on the garage, he improvises a different life for his father. He sings, he dances, he scribbles poems in the air, and he attempts a cartwheel, which, he realizes too late, is not something you should do on a frozen, slippery garage roof.

Then Leo tries to make his own lists.

A. High School
   1. To get the lead in a play and not *glurt*.

There's only one thing on the list, and that one thing took Leo a half hour to come up with. It seems to show a lack of initiative. He keeps thinking of things that are more immediate or have nothing to do with school:

   1. To get through the play, *Rumpopo's Porch*, without glurting.
   2. To find out about Rosaria and why no one talks about her.

3. To be Leo, not the *sardine,* not *fog boy.*
4. To find out what I am good at.
5. For my father to be happy again, for everything to be *okay.*

And when Leo writes the last one, he feels unsettled and edgy, as if it is such an urgent mission, and such an impossible one.

Leo forces himself to think of abandoned children, like the ones in *Rumpopo's Porch,* children who have nothing, but still they don't complain, and they imagine the most wonderful things, and they make other people happy when they do this.

Leo rips up his lists.

He tries a "Life" list, and suddenly he is full of high ideals:

1. To save the sick and starving children.
2. To stop war.
3. To save the environment.

Leo stops. He thinks of all the amazing things a person could try to do, but they seem too big, all those things, and so he scratches them out and writes:

1. To be a father.

And again he feels uneasy, because he isn't sure he means it. To be a father seems unimaginable, and at the same time, it does not look as important as the other things he listed, and he is ashamed because he knows it *should be* extremely important.

Chores

Today, when Leo's mother says (for the nine millionth time) "Aye yie yie! My life is slave and errand girl!" Leo thinks about that. He knows she always has a lot to do, but none of it seemed too hard until his father had his heart attack. Leo would find her crying in the kitchen, only she'd pretend she hadn't been crying. She'd start to wash a pot and would just stare out the window, her shoulders sagging, as if she were carrying an elephant on her back.

She made lists, endless lists: of groceries to buy, bills to be paid, things to fix, doctors' appointments, dentist appointments, little lists everywhere you turned. As soon as some items would be checked off a list, new ones would be scribbled in. She marked off the days on the calendar that was posted by the phone: black slashes when each day was done, and when the month was done, *rippp,* she'd tear the page off the calendar and smash it into a ball and toss it in the trash.

One day Leo's father found her crying while she was cleaning the toilet. He called everyone together. "How many people are in this house?" he asked.

Contento said, "Gosh, Papa, you know that. Six."

"And how many people use this toilet?"

Pietro made a gagging sound, followed by "Geez. Yuk."

Nunzio clapped his hands, as if this were a game. "All of uth! All of uth uthe it!"

Papa said, "What I want to know is this: if there are six people in this house, and if six people use this toilet, why is there only one person—your mother—who cleans it?"

"Uh-oh," Leo said.

Contento flapped her arms, as if dismissing the subject. "We don't know how. She cleans the best."

Pietro agreed. "I don't know the first thing about it."

"Well, guess what?" Papa said. "Everybody's going to learn. Now. Everybody's going to take a turn. Even me."

Pietro said, "Barf."

This started a snowball of scenes which always began with Papa saying, "How many people are in this house?" And that would be followed by, on one day, "And how many people wear clothes? And how many of those clothes get dirty? And need washing?" On another day, "How many people are in this house? And how many people eat? And how many dishes get dirty?"

Maybe that makes it better for Leo's mother. Sometimes, Leo hears her on the phone with one of her old friends, and she will be laughing, and her voice will sound girlish and happy, and he sees her feet tapping on the floor, a little dance as she sits in the chair.

━━●

Leo is holding a press conference. He is explaining his revolutionary discoveries. The first is a fully automated house-cleaner robot.

"It's amazing," one reporter says. "It cleans toilets, washes clothes, does dishes, prepares meals! Who or what inspired this astounding invention?"

Leo looks thoughtful, places one hand to his chin. "My mother," he said. "I owe it all to my mother."

The audience says, "Awww."

"And this second discovery," another reporter says, "a cure for heart attacks. No one will ever have another heart attack?"

The reporters are in a frenzy.

"It's a miracle!"

"Astounding!"

Leo looks out at the audience, and there in the back, he sees his parents, smiling and holding hands. His father looks the picture of health.

A man hands Leo a cell phone. "It's urgent," the man whispers.

"Yes?" Leo says. "The Nobel Prize? Why, thank you. What inspired me to pursue this research? Hmm. I did it for my parents. Yes, that's right. I did it for my parents." And Leo looks out across the crowd and sees his father and mother beaming.

Discussions

R uby and Leo leave rehearsal while Rumpopo/ Orlando and Lucia/Melanie are still arguing. Rumpopo was insisting that his character was responsible for all the magical happenings, while Lucia insisted it was her character.

"So who do you agree with?" Ruby asks. "Rumpopo or Lucia?"

"Rumpopo. I think. Yeah, definitely Rumpopo, because he tells the stories, right?"

"But the children act them out," Ruby says.

"But they couldn't act them out if they didn't have his stories."

Ruby stops, puts her face up close to Leo's. "So why doesn't anything magical happen when he's all alone, like at the beginning?"

"You smell like oranges," Leo says. "Why is that?"

She sniffs her wrist. "I dunno. Maybe it's my lotion."

"It's a good smell."

"Thanks. So what do you think?" Ruby says. "If Rumpopo makes the magic, how come nothing magical happens when he's alone?"

"I don't know."

"Well, here's what I think," Ruby says. "I think he *needs* the children, that there's something about them—"

"Well, maybe. But they need him, too, right?"

"Yeah," Ruby says. "I guess you're right."

"Me? Right?"

Mr. Beeber assembles the cast for a discussion of the play. He feels that they need a chance "to air concerns and questions about various elements." Leo hopes they will discuss what the play is really about. Instead:

LUCIA: Will we be using a real dog? If so, can we use mine?

RUMPOPO: Why would we use *your* dog? We

	should use *my* dog. It's a golden—
LUCIA:	No way, that dog's too big.
MR. BEEBER:	Cast! Please! I have already chosen the dog—
LUCIA:	Which one? Whose is it? It's not a pit bull, is it?
MR. BEEBER:	Cast! Please! I was hoping this would be a chance to discuss elements of the play. Does anyone have any questions about—
RUMPOPO:	Yeah. I have one. Why is the dog in the play anyway? I mean really.
LUCIA:	Exactly. Maybe we don't have to mess with the dog.
RUMPOPO:	If we're going to take out the dog, we should take out the donkey, too.
DONKEY:	*Ex-cuse* me?
LUCIA:	Well, really, what does the donkey add?
RUMPOPO:	The villagers and the old crone are just extras anyway—
OLD CRONE:	Extras? Extras?
RUMPOPO:	I'll tell you who is an extra—that donkey—

MR. BEEBER: Cast! Cast! Please!

Leo lies on the floor, the play script over his face. Mr. Beeber makes an announcement. He is getting rid of Rumpopo and Lucia, and the new play revolves around the old crone, the donkey, and the villagers. News of this play travels far and wide. The phone rings. It's Broadway calling.

"Leo? We're taking this play to Broadway. You're the only one who can do the part of the old crone."

"Well—"

"We need you, Leo."

"Well—"

"Please, Leo—"

"Well, okay. I'll do it."

On the morning after opening night, the headlines read: "Revolutionary New Play!" and "Leo Transfixes the Audience!" and "The Old Crone Rules!"

The phone rings. It's a reporter.

"Leo, how were you able to transform yourself so completely into an old crone?"

"I'm not sure. I just tried to imagine what she might feel like."

"Remarkable!"

<hr>

"That's all for today, cast. Leo? You awake over there?"

"Huh? Oh. Yeah." Leo watches Mr. Beeber gather his papers. "Mr. Beeber? Why'd you write this play?"

Mr. Beeber turns to Leo. "I just wanted to. It was fun to do."

"But why *this* play?"

"How do you mean?"

"Why this particular play, about Rumpopo and the children and the stories? Did some of this happen to you? Are you like Rumpopo?"

Mr. Beeber stacks his papers on a side table. "Hmm." He studies Leo's face. "Interesting question, that. Hard to answer. None of it happened to me exactly, not the way it is in the play, no."

"But then why did you think of it?"

"I guess I was thinking of my father. He's old, like Rumpopo, and he was a sad, old grouchy man."

"And did something happen—did some abandoned kids come to stay with him?"

Mr. Beeber smiles and scratches his neck. "No, not that exactly. He came to live with us—with me and my wife and our two children."

"And does he tell them stories, like Rumpopo does?"

"Yes, he does."

"And do they make him feel young again?"

Mr. Beeber looks thoughtful, his eyes focused on something in the distance. "Yes, they do."

"So who's the old crone?"

"Pardon?"

"The old crone in the play—is she like anyone you know?"

"Ha! Good question. I don't know. Maybe a little like me?"

"Huh."

The Microscope

Leo walks all the way home with Ruby in order to help her carry her science project. Leo doesn't know why she's lugging it home, why she didn't just toss it in the rubbish at school. It's an ungainly mess of plastic cups with half-dead plants, part of a photosynthesis display.

"I know what you're thinking," Ruby says. "You're wondering why I'm keeping all this junk, right?"

"Well—"

"Admit it, it's a miserable-looking muddle." Ruby frowns at her plants.

"But your report was great, Ruby."

Ruby shifts the bundle in her arms. "I grew sort of attached to these straggly plants."

Ruby's mother is waiting at the door. "Hey there, Ruby babe! Hey there, Leonardo da Vinci! Want some cake?"

Ruby's mother sits at the table with them and asks Leo about his science project.

"I'm not the world's best scientist," Leo says.

"You *might* be!" she says. "Maybe you just don't know it yet."

"I hate science projects," Leo admits.

Ruby's mother leans toward Leo. "Know what? So did I, when I was your age. I was so glad Ruby came up with this idea on her own. So what'd you do?"

Ruby smiles. "Go on, tell her."

"The solar system."

"No!" Ruby's mother says. "Not really? That's what I did, too!"

"That's what every kid does," Leo says, "who hates science projects."

Ruby's mother laughs. She thinks it's hilarious.

Later, while Ruby is watering her droopy plants, Leo says, "You're lucky to be the only kid in your family."

She sucks in her breath.

"No wait, sorry, I didn't mean—that must sound really stupid and awful. I wasn't thinking about your brother—I mean—"

"What *did* you mean, Leo?"

"I meant that your mother notices you're there. You're not just one of a band of goats."

"Goats?"

"She *appreciates* you."

"Oh. Well, yeah. But listen, Leo, sometimes it's hard being the only kid. It's like I'm under a microscope. They notice every little thing I do. Sometimes I'd like to be *anonymous.* Not always, but sometimes."

"Huh." It had never before occurred to Leo that there might be some advantages to feeling anonymous.

Ruby touches the stem of one of her plants. "It's okay," she says to the plant, "you'll be fine." As she rearranges the plants on the windowsill, she says, "Who's the gardener in your family? Who grows all those flowers and vegetables in your backyard?"

"My father."

"Really?"

"Really. Most people think my mother does all that, but she doesn't."

"It's a pretty amazing garden."

"You think?" Leo has spent so much time avoiding Papa's requests to help with the weeding that he's never thought about what the garden might look like to others.

One whole side of the yard is a bank of peony bushes that bloom enormous pink blossoms in June. Surrounding the birdbath are Papa's rose-bushes, about twenty of them, which he seems to coax into bloom each summer, bending over them, spraying them, gently removing the fully opened roses before the petals fall. Flanking the other side of the yard is his vegetable garden, in which he grows corn, lettuce, beans, peas, cucumbers, and his special pride—fat, juicy tomatoes.

In the spring and summer, Papa is out there first thing in the morning and immediately after dinner each night. Leo thinks of himself in the maple tree and the attic, and he wonders if the garden is where Papa goes to have quiet.

Ruby says, "You're the one who should have done this photosynthesis display. Maybe you've got your father's green thumb."

"Nah," Leo says. "I don't know the first thing about it." But he wonders how his father learned, and if Papa might have been proud if Leo had done a science project like Ruby's.

As Leo is leaving, his eyes are drawn to a photo on the hall table. A younger Ruby is hugging a little boy with red curly hair, like Ruby's. "Is that—?"

"Yes," Ruby says. "That's my brother. Johnny. Cute, huh?"

"Yeah."

All the way home, Leo can't get that picture out of his mind. There was this real boy, Johnny, and he was Ruby's brother, and now he is gone. Gone. Leo can't imagine either of his brothers or his sister gone, even though Pietro and Contento are sometimes annoying. He doesn't want to think of the word *dead*; it is too awful. To have someone you love go—it must leave a big, empty hole in yourself, and no one can see the hole, only you.

Chili Bear

Saturday morning, home alone for two whole hours! Leo is curled on the sofa, reading about Rosaria in Papa's *Autobiography, Age of Thirteen.*

> *Rosaria is the youngest and everyone's favorite. She carries a fuzzy red bear with her everywhere. Its name is Chili Bear. She'll say "Chili Bear needs a cookie," and "Chili Bear needs a hug," and "Chili Bear does not want to take a bath"—which means that* she *needs a cookie or a hug or doesn't want a bath. She'll push that little bear in your face and say, "Don't you just* love *Chili Bear?"*

In a photograph that appears at the end of this chapter, the whole family is seated on a blanket, at a picnic. They are bundled up, and most of them are smiling at the camera. Two of the boys are not smiling; they seem to be pinching each other. Leo can tell which are his grandparents, of course, and which is his father, and Auntie Maddalena (because she has light hair, unlike the others) and Uncle Guido (who has a very large head, still does). Leo looks for Rosaria. That must be her, the smallest one, on Grandma Navy's lap. Sure enough, there's a stuffed bear in her hand. Rosaria gazes directly into the camera with deep, deep dark eyes.

As Leo is about to close Papa's book, something in that picture catches his eye. In the background, behind and off to one side of the family, is a little white dog. It's not looking at the camera, but at the family, or maybe at the cake that Grandpa Navy is holding on his lap.

In the attic, Leo grabs the tap shoes, and off he goes, skittering across the floor and wondering if that little white dog belonged to the family or if it just happened by as their picture was being taken. What happened to Rosaria, and why is Leo not allowed to mention her name? Where is that "favorite one," the one with the Chili Bear?

The Relatives Return

It's Sunday morning, and Leo is pretending to be asleep. Mom and Contento are in the hallway.

"But, Mom, Mom, listen," Contento says. "Write it down. You'll forget. The game is next week—"

Nunzio, who is still in bed, shouts out, "Mom! Mom! The moothic fethtival ith next week—I have a tholo—write it down!"

Pietro joins in, from his bed. "Mom! Mom! You and Papa promised you'd come to my football game on Friday. You *promised*. You haven't been to a single one yet. Write it down!"

Leo is about to add his two cents' worth, to remind them about the play coming up, when Mom appears at their bedroom door.

"Look at you, lazy band of goats. Get up! And

clean this filthy pigsty room and then come down and help me in the kitchen."

Pietro moans. "What? Why?"

Mom is already hustling down the hall as she says, "Grandma and Grandpa and the aunties and uncles and cousins are coming—"

Pietro says, "Barf. Talk about a band of goats."

Later, in the kitchen:

Mom is in frantic mode. "Aye yie yie! Sardine-o, run next door and borrow some flour, and Contento, go iron the tablecloth, no, not that one—"

Nunzio pokes his head in the doorway. "Mom, Mom, Pietro ith on the roof."

"What? Aye yie yie. Get your papa—"

Later, on the porch:

Auntie Angela, arms crossed, says, "I'm not going in."

Uncle Guido says, "Oh, come on, Angela—"

In the front hallway:

Auntie Maddalena is fuming. "If Angela weren't my sister, I'd strangle her."

Mom says, "Don't talk like that."

"Don't tell me how to talk."

On the back porch:

Cousin Tina is kicking at the door. "Why do we have to come *here?* I hate to come here."

Cousin Joey says, "Me, too. Land of the boring."

In the kitchen:

Grandma Navy is looking in all the pots. "Rice?" she says. "Mariana made rice? What's she got against potatoes, I'd like to know? And where's my Carlo?"

Auntie Carmella bats her hand at a fly. "Traveling. Of course."

"He travels too much. And your husband?"

"Golfing. Of course."

"He golfs too much."

In the garage:

Grandpa Navy is inspecting the headlights of Papa's car. "You got a new car?"

Papa says, "No, it's the same one you saw last time."

Grandpa taps on the hood. "I've had my car for twelve years. If you take care of them, they last forever, you know."

Papa studies the ceiling. "I know," he says. "I know."

Dinner is served:

When Papa says he'd like to propose a toast, Grandpa says, "*Mangia!* Let's eat. I'm so hungry I could eat a horse."

Uncle Paolo, who has not yet said a word, says to the air, "Are we having—"

Maddalena continues for him. "Rice? Of course

we are having rice. Mariana *always* serves rice. You ought to know that by now."

From the kids' table:

Cousin Tina whines, "Mom, Mom, Pietro is eating with his hands."

Pietro says, "Tattletale turkey."

"Thtop it," Nunzio says to Joey, who has pinched him.

At the big table:

Auntie Carmella jabs her bread stick at Mom and says, "Mariana, are you ever going to do anything about Nunzio's lisp? You need to send him to a speech therapist."

At the kids' table:

Cousin Tina says, "Hey sardine, old witch, you got a broom in that play? A broom to fly on?"

The big table:

Grandma says, "Where're the potatoes?"

Leo gets up to get more bread from the big table, and when Auntie Carmella hands him the bread basket, Leo says, "Auntie Carmella, did you and Papa and everybody ever have a dog?"

Auntie Carmella gasps. "Leo!"

Papa says, "Leo!"

Grandma Navy rushes off to the bathroom. "Oh, oh, oh!"

In the kitchen:

Papa says, "What has come over you? How do you manage to upset your grandmother every time she comes here?"

"But what'd I say? All I asked was—"

"I know exactly what you asked. Who put you up to that? Was it Auntie Angela?"

"I—I—"

"It was, wasn't it?"

"I—I—"

"Go back to the table. And keep your mouth closed, you hear?"

And Leo does. He keeps his mouth closed throughout the rest of the meal and all evening long. He says not one tiny word. Maybe he will never speak again.

A large yellow sign appears on Leo's front door: QUARANTINED. They are not allowed to have any guests (especially relatives) over ever again.

A doctor comes to examine Leo. He says to Leo's parents, "And you say he just stopped talking? One day he talked, and the next day he didn't?"

Leo's mom wrings her hands. "Yes," she says. "That's right."

"And you have no idea why? There was nothing traumatic?"

"Well," says Papa, "I might have said something—"

"Like what?" Mom says. "What did you say now?"

Papa looks sheepish, hangs his head.

The doctor examines Leo's throat. "Hmm," he says. "Hmm. I think you might try some chocolate brownies and ice cream. That might do the trick."

Leo smiles, but he does not speak. He'll wait for the brownies and the ice cream.

Crash, Smash, Crumple

It is bitter cold as the family piles in the car to go to Pietro's football game.

PIETRO: Hurry up! I'm going to be late. The coach is going to kill me.

MOM: Contento! Contento? Where is that girl?

NUNZIO: I lotht my thoothe.

MOM: Your what?

NUNZIO: My thoothe.

PAPA: Well, go find them!

LEO: Who took my gloves?

PIETRO: The coach is going to *kill* me.

When they finally get to the game, the coach is ready to *kill* Pietro. The other team looks awfully big: huge, hulking creatures. Pietro straggles onto the field, his shoulder pads flopping on his shoulders like enormous ungainly wings, his shins appearing pale and skinny and vulnerable.

Leo is not a big fan of football, but he has learned to pretend.

Someone kicks the ball. *Crash, smash, crumple.* They're all down. Someone passes the ball. *Crash, smash, crumple.* They're all down.

Leo's mother is clapping, and Papa beams at the man next to him. "That's my son Pietro out there!"

They all yell "Rah, rah, Pietro," even though they can't see him, buried in the piles of bodies.

On the third play, they see him. He is the one lying there, not getting up. They carry him off on a stretcher. He broke his leg.

In the hospital waiting room, while Mom and Pietro are with the doctors, Papa hunches forward in a chair, wiping his palms on his khaki trousers. He says, "That boy was doing pretty well out there on the field."

"Yep," Leo agrees.

"Too bad about the leg, though."

"Yep. Papa? His leg will be all right, won't it?"

"Sure," Papa says. "Sure it will." He wipes his palms on his trousers again.

At home, Pietro seems proud of his cast, but he looks shaken and lies on his bed staring at the ceiling. Leo offers him a candy bar he has kept hidden in the closet.

"Thanks," Pietro says, tearing off the wrapper and nibbling at the candy.

"Does it hurt, your leg?"

Pietro reaches down and pats the cast. "A little."

"Papa said you were playing really well out there."

"He did?" Pietro grins. "Well, I would've done a lot better if I hadn't broken my stupid leg."

"Yeah."

The crowds are cheering, a thunderous roar rising in the stadium. Coach Leo signals to Pietro, the quarterback. At the next play, Pietro deftly drops back, fades right, and there! He has the ball. He's taking it down the field. Touchdown! The crowd goes wild. They've won the championship!

Reporters surround Coach Leo and his star player, Pietro.

"Coach, how do you feel about your team today?"

"Great! It was a team effort all the way."

"And Pietro, how did you feel about the game?"

"We were ready. We did our best. We've got a great coach."

Coach Leo sees Papa on the sidelines. "Papa, come here."

Papa seems shy as he walks over to join his boys.

"Are these your sons?" the reporter asks.

"Yes," Papa says, leaning into the microphone.

"You must be proud of them today."

"Yes," Papa agrees. "I am. Very, very proud."

Splat

It is sleeting, icy sharp needles bombarding the family as they pile in the car to go to Contento's soccer game.

CONTENTO: Hurry up! I'm going to be late. The coach is going to kill me.
MOM: Pietro! Pietro? Where is that boy?
NUNZIO: I lotht my thoothe.

The coach is ready to *kill* Contento. The other team looks so much older and bigger than Contento's: giant girls with rippling muscles. Contento runs onto the field, her shirt streaked with mud before the game has begun, but she looks good out there, all rosy-cheeked and black curls bobbing.

Leo's mother's smile is so wide. Papa says, to

the woman in front of him, "That's my daughter, Contento, out there!" He's *smiling*.

Leo doesn't understand soccer, but he pretends.

The whistle blows, someone kicks the ball, everybody runs, someone else gets the ball, everyone runs the other way, someone else gets the ball, back and forth, up and down the field. Leo feels tired just watching. He tries to focus on Contento but loses her in the field of running girls. But there, there, she aims for the goal! It is blocked. They all run the other way. Back and forth, back and forth. Leo and his family all cheer whenever they feel like it: "Rah, rah, Contento! Go, go, Contento!"

And then, spectacularly, Contento has the ball and is taking it down the field, way ahead of her opponents. For a moment, Leo sees the appeal of sports: the grace in running, the skills perfected, the teamwork. Leo thinks of the play he's in, when one character passes a line to the next, who runs with it.

The family cheers like mad for Contento racing down the field, and then, *whoosh,* she slips in the mud, her legs fly out from under her, and for a moment she is suspended there in the air, and then, *splat,* she comes down hard, and she lies there, writhing and moaning.

They carry her off on a stretcher. She has dislocated her knee.

In the hospital waiting room, a nurse says to Papa, "Weren't you just in here yesterday?" As Papa nods, the nurse spies Pietro with his cast and crutches. She narrows her eyes at Papa, as if she suspects him of beating his children.

"It's my daughter this time. Soccer," Papa says. "She's a very good player." He then motions to Pietro. "Football."

The nurse looks at Leo and Nunzio. "And what torturous games do you two play?"

Nunzio says, "Nothing! I thing!"

"Thing?"

"Sing," clarifies Papa.

"And I'm in a play," Leo adds.

"Well, good," says the nurse. "Then we won't be seeing you two in here, will we?"

"Oh no," Nunzio says. "Never!"

At home, Contento is irritable, frustrated with her knee and crutches. "It hurts," she moans. "Hurts like crazy!"

When Leo brings her cookies and iced tea, Contento bursts into tears. "That's just so, so nice." She nibbles at the cookies, sniffling.

"Papa said you're a really good soccer player."

Contento's eyes open wide. "He *did*? He said that?"

"Yes, and he was grinning like mad when you were on the field."

"He *was*?"

Now the crowd is roaring for Coach Leo and his star women's soccer team. The stadium is packed, everyone cheering and waving banners. And there goes Contento, racing down the field, her toes seeming to barely touch the ball, as if the ball is leading her down the field, and she aims, *whop*, and the ball slides into the net under the outstretched arm of the goalie. They've won!

The team carries Contento and Coach Leo on their shoulders, splashing champagne on their heads, and the crowd pours onto the field like a giant wave.

Agony

L oud thunder and pouring rain as they pile in the car to go to Nunzio's music festival.

NUNZIO: Hurry up! I'm going to be late. My teacher ith going to *kill* me.

MOM: Pietro! Contento? Where *are* they?

PIETRO: How do you expect me to hurry with these clumsy crutches?

CONTENTO: *Your* clumsy crutches. What about *my* clumsy crutches?

NUNZIO: My thoothe—

In the car, everyone gets poked with crutches. When they reach the school, for the music festival, Grandma and Grandpa Navy are waiting in the lobby. They look annoyed.

Grandma Navy says, "What took you so long?"

Grandpa Navy points toward the auditorium. "They wouldn't let us save seats."

"For grandparents, they don't reserve seats?" Grandma asks.

Nunzio rushes off to his classroom, where the teacher is ready to *kill* him. Leo's family looks for seats, poking people with crutches. "Excuse us. Sorry. Excuse us. Oops, sorry." They get stuck in the back of the room, behind tall people with hats.

Grandma says, "For grandparents, they should reserve seats."

The festival begins with the youngest students, cute little five-year-old cherubs fidgeting with their clothes and waving at their families. Everyone loves them. They don't even have to sing. All they have to do is stand there wriggling, and people will applaud.

The first and second graders follow, and then the third graders, Nunzio's class, file onto the stage. They are trying to be grown-up, attempting to stand straight on the risers, and their eyes are on their teacher (most of the time), who looks very serious. They sing one short song, and then in the next one, Nunzio has his solo, and his voice is astounding, soaring through the auditorium, so clear and pure, like an angel singing. The audience is hushed as they listen to the amazing Nunzio, and both Mom and Grandma Navy are dabbing at their eyes with tissues. Papa taps the man in front of him. "That's my son Nunzio!" he says. His smile is *huge*.

Leo sees in his mind an image of his father and mother, spinning off pieces of themselves: Contento, Nunzio, Pietro, and Leo. And Leo wonders if dreams can change, and if he and his brothers and sister are the new dreams of Papa, and is that enough, and is that better than the other dreams he had?

When Nunzio's song ends, everyone applauds like crazy. The family leaps up, shouting, "*Bravo, bravo*, Nunzio!" and Nunzio's class is grinning and bowing, and then there is some sort of commotion on the row above Nunzio. Two boys from the top row tumble into the children in the row below, and then those children tumble into the next row, and legs and arms are everywhere, and someone is crying, and then many children are crying.

There is total pandemonium in the auditorium, despite the principal's attempts to encourage everyone to remain calm. Parents are rushing to the stage, children are jumping off the stage, the little ones in the audience are crying and wailing.

Fortunately, only two children have to be carted out on stretchers. Unfortunately, one of them is Nunzio. Blood trickles from his forehead, and he is unconscious. Grandma Navy takes one look at Nunzio and staggers. She regains her balance and leans down to caress Nunzio's foot. For a moment, Leo fears that she, too, will be carted out on a stretcher.

They are all floundering. Mom and Papa rush off in the ambulance with Nunzio while Contento, Pietro (and their crutches) and Leo pile in the car with Grandma and Grandpa Navy, following them to the hospital. On the way through the dark night to the hospital, Leo is praying for Nunzio-bunzio and making all kinds of bargains with God, if He will only make Nunzio okay. It seems to Leo that this is an awful lot of bad luck for one family in one week, and that you could never put this kind of thing in a play, because people wouldn't believe it.

—◆—

Leo, famous physicist, faces a bank of reporters. The camera lights are blinding. Hundreds of black microphones loom in front of his face.

A breathless reporter says, "You've discovered how to stop and even reverse time? Is that really true?"

"Yes," Leo says. "For instance, we can now rewind it. Let's say someone is injured. We can rewind time to just before each injury and replay it so that no one gets hurt."

"Think of the implications!" a reporter says.

"You could undo car crashes!"

"Accidents of all sorts!"

"War!"

"Yes," Leo agrees. He nods humbly.

"Phenomenal!"

Leo's publicist appears at his side, whispers

into his ear, and hands him a cell phone.

"Yes?" Leo says. "Another Nobel Prize? Why, thank you. Thank you very much. I am deeply honored."

The Album

A much-too-early snowstorm arrives. Leo stands on the porch, scanning the snow-covered steps and yard, blinking in the white brightness of the day. Deep silence all around, except for the distant *scrape, scrape* of a snow shovel down the block. Leo leaps, *whoosh,* snow flying up around him, streaks across the yard and up the maple tree, not so easy in a winter coat and boots and gloves. He looks back at his house, at its snow-covered roof, the lights within, his footprints on the porch.

Down the tree, jump, *thud,* over the rhododendron bush, scattering snow from its top, squeezing between house and hedge, speeding down one side of the yard, around the birdbath, taking his usual route, thinking all the time about Nunzio. He has a concussion and swelling of his brain, but he is conscious and, except for the occasional vomiting and a "mathive" headache, he seems a little better today. He even sang for the nurses when Leo was visiting him.

Leo scrambles up the pear tree and pauses on the top of the garage, squatting in the snow. Nunzio has scared everyone. Papa and Mom stayed with him at the hospital the first night, and Contento, Pietro, and Leo went home with Grandma and Grandpa Navy. They were quiet and somber, sitting together on Grandma and Grandpa Navy's sofa, not even poking one another. Leo wanted to ask "Could he *die?*" but he was afraid, as if to say it would make it possible, but if he didn't say it, it would not be possible.

It reminded Leo of how he felt when Papa was in the hospital, how afraid he was, and he realizes now, that he is *still* afraid for Papa. *What if he has another heart attack? What if I can't save him?*

Leo scrambles over the side of the garage, drops, *poof,* and races back to the porch. Again he leaps, and starts another round.

After they sit in silence at Grandma and Grandpa's for some time, Contento starts bawling, which makes Pietro bawl, which makes Leo bawl.

Grandma is flustered. "What? What? Don't cry!"

Grandpa says, "Maybe we should eat something—"

Pietro wipes his nose on his sleeve and says, "Nunzio is going to die!"

Both Grandma and Grandpa say, "No, no—"

Contento whimpers, "Don't let him die."

Grandpa Navy hurries into the kitchen and returns with a bowl of peppermint candies. "Here, here, have candy."

"Don't cry," Grandma says. "Nunzio will be fine."

"Have candy," Grandpa urges.

Leo drags himself off the couch, wanders to the bookshelf, runs his fingers along the spines. On the bottom shelf is a row of albums. He pulls one out, flips through the photos, puts it back, withdraws another, and returns to the sofa, where Contento and Pietro are still sniffling. Grandpa is eating candy. Leo hears a small intake of breath from Grandma as he opens the album. She eases herself onto the sofa between Leo and Contento, and her hand hovers in the air, as if she might stop Leo, but she doesn't.

Leo turns several pages, stopping at a photograph of Grandma and Grandpa seated on a blanket outside, with their children gathered around them. It is the same photograph that is in Papa's *Autobiography, Age of Thirteen*. As Grandpa Navy unwraps another candy, he looks agitated, nervous. He walks over to the window and stares out.

Leo says, "Grandma, tell me who everyone is in this picture."

Grandma Navy clears her throat and slowly identifies everyone in the picture, all her children, one by one. The last one she points to is the little girl on her lap. "And this," she says, "this is Rosaria."

Leo says, "Rosaria!"

Contento and Pietro look puzzled. "Rosaria?"

Grandma Navy turns a few more pages, as if something has come over her, some urgency. "And this is Rosaria," she says, pointing to a slightly older Rosaria, and a few pages later, she says, "And this is Rosaria," and on she goes through the album, showing them all the pictures of Rosaria. In the last one Grandma turns to, Rosaria seems about sixteen or seventeen years old, a little older than Contento. She is sitting on the porch, in a navy blue dress, and she is looking off to one side, at something just outside the picture frame, and she is smiling.

It is quiet in the living room. Leo turns the pages back to the first one. "And that," he says, pointing to the dog in the background, "was that your dog?"

Grandma Navy leans toward the picture, presses her lips together, and nods. "It was Rosaria's dog," she says.

Rosaria

Grandma turns the pages of the album again, and this time she tells them about Rosaria. Leo can see from the photographs that Rosaria is a happy child, and Grandma confirms this. "Such a laugh Rosaria had, a deep and hearty *ha ha ha*, and whenever she laughed, everyone around her would have to laugh." And Rosaria had a way of looking at you, Grandma Navy says, that made you feel as if she understood what you were thinking, as if she knew everything there was to know about you.

"And how she loved to dance!" Grandma says, turning to Grandpa. "Remember?"

"Mmm."

"Her little feet, tapping all the time." Grandma Navy touches Rosaria's feet in the photograph. She turns the page. Rosaria is standing on their porch, her mouth wide open. "And sing! Oh, she loved to sing, too!" Again she turns to Grandpa. "Remember?"

"Mmm."

"And here, see this one? She's acting out a little play with your papa. That's his hat she's wearing."

Leo leans toward the photograph. "Papa? Doing plays?"

Grandma says, "Oh yes, your papa loved to do plays. He turned everything into a play."

"Papa?"

Why didn't Papa write about this in his autobiography? Leo tries to remember Papa's list of goals. He doesn't think being an actor was one of them. If not, why not?

Grandma returns to the first photograph. Her finger strays across the photo, to the little dog. "And Rosaria loved that little dog, how she loved—" Her voice catches, and she stops. Grandpa turns from his place at the window and comes to her. He takes the album gently, as if it might dissolve in his hands, and he stares at the picture.

Contento says, "What happened—"

Pietro interrupts. "—to Rosaria?"

And Leo blurts, "Something bad?"

Grandpa Navy closes the album, returns it to the shelf. With his back to them, he says, "She left. We don't see her anymore."

Grandma Navy ushers them to the kitchen, urging them to sit down and eat soup, as if that will fortify them. They sit around the table, slurping soup, and this time it is Grandpa who continues the story.

"Rosaria and your papa were very close, like this," he says, placing the palms of his hands together. "One day, her little dog dies, her precious little dog."

Grandma sniffles when he mentions the dog.

"And Rosaria is inconsolable. She will talk to no one, only your papa. And he tries his best, you know, he tries to comfort her. He even makes a little play about a young woman and her dog, something to cheer her up, remember that?" He looks at Grandma, who nods. "There is also the boyfriend," Grandpa says, glancing at Grandma again.

"Ack, the boyfriend!" she says.

"And while Rosaria is still being inconsolable about her dog, we get into an argument."

"Over the boyfriend," Grandma adds. "The stupid boyfriend."

"And I don't know why or how exactly, but Rosaria one day she packs up and leaves. We didn't even know until the next day."

"With the boyfriend?" Contento asks. "Did she go off with the boyfriend?"

"Yes," Grandpa says.

"The stupid boyfriend," Grandma says, again.

They sit there and look at their hands.

"And then?" Leo says. "What happened?"

Grandpa taps his spoon against the table in a steady drumbeat as he answers. "We get a letter, says they're married—"

"Married!" Contento says.

"Don't you get any ideas," Grandma says to her. "Don't you ever run off without telling your parents."

Contento stares down at her bowl.

"But that's not so bad, right?" Leo says. "I mean, so she's married—"

"Not so bad?" Grandma says. "Well, maybe it doesn't sound so bad to you, and maybe we would have got used to the idea, but the boyfriend was not a good person, and we wouldn't accept him, and Rosaria refused to come home."

"Ever?" Contento asks.

"Well, once she came," Grandpa says.

"It was not good," Grandma says. "It was a couple years later. The boyfriend—the husband—was long gone, but Rosaria was different. She argued with us over every little thing. She said we didn't know her! Imagine that! Telling your parents they don't know you! Who knows you better than your parents, I ask you, who?"

"But maybe," Leo says, "maybe she felt, with all the kids in the family, that she was, I don't know, like, invisible or something—"

"Invisible!" Grandma says, slapping her hand against the table, making them all jump. "Invisible? None of my children was ever invisible, I can tell you that!"

And then she starts to cry, and both Contento and Pietro look at Leo, accusingly, and he apologizes to Grandma, but she leaves the table, saying, "Oh, oh, oh."

Grandpa sits there, staring at his spoon, as if it's

a crystal ball that shows the past, not the future. He says, "It's difficult. We don't see her, hear from her. We miss her." He looks at Leo, right into his eyes, and he does not say anything, but it seems to Leo as if maybe, yes, Grandpa still hopes and wishes and dreams that Rosaria will come home someday. And maybe Papa does, too.

Leo is struggling through deep snow in dense woods. The bitterly cold wind howls around him, blowing snow into his face, obscuring the path. It is dark, with only the occasional stream of moonlight glancing off the snow. Leo is not sure how much longer he can go on. He stumbles, falls. But he must go on; he *must*.

At last he sees the tumbledown cabin, snow piled against its door. A light shines in one of the windows.

Leo pounds on the door.

A woman, huddled in a wool blanket, pries open the door a few inches.

Leo studies her for a moment. "Rosaria?" he says.

"Yes?"

"I am your nephew Leo."

"Oh! How did you find me?"

"I have ways."

Rosaria lets him in, and he explains his mission. Rosaria weeps. She wants to come home but is afraid. Leo reassures her, tells her that everyone misses her and wants to see her.

In the morning, Leo leads Rosaria out through the snow, and she returns with Leo to Grandma and Grandpa's house. Rosaria is so happy to be home, at last! And Grandma and Grandpa Navy and Papa and all the aunties and uncles can hardly believe it. Rosaria is home!

—

"Hey, fog boy! Earth to fog boy! Do you want more soup or not?"

That night, Leo and Pietro sleep upstairs in the room that used to be their father's and Uncle Guido's. Leo has been in this room before, but not often. Dangling on the back of the door are red and blue baseball caps. GIORGIO THE GREAT is scrawled in pen on one of the visors. On the dressers stand gleaming trophies, some for Giorgio, some for Guido. Two framed diplomas hang side by side on one wall. Leo guesses these might have been added after his papa and Guido left home. They don't look like something boys would hang in their rooms. On the opposite wall are framed photos of the four brothers together, of the whole family, and one of the great-grandparents, who look serious and stern in their black clothes. These, too, Leo thinks, must have been added more recently, just like the crisp blue bedspreads.

Leo climbs into one of the twin beds. Had this been Papa's bed? He stares up at the ceiling with its domed light fixture. What had Papa been thinking when he lay in his bed all those nights? Leo glances toward the single window, framed in blue curtains, to his right. The shade is up, and he can see the bare branches of a tree, and beyond them, the house across the street with one light on upstairs.

Grandma Navy taps at their door, entering shyly. "You boys okay?" she asks.

Pietro grunts, already half asleep. Leo says, "Sure."

Grandma walks to the window and pulls down the shade.

"Grandma?" Leo says. "I'm sorry if I keep upsetting you. I don't mean to."

Grandma turns. "*You* don't upset me. Rosaria upsets me," she says. "But you know something? It was a little good to talk about her tonight, to look at those pictures. It upset me, yes, but it was a little good, too."

"Can I ask you something?"

"What?"

"Do you think Nunzio will be okay?"

"For certain!" Grandma says. "He will be hunky-dory. Don't you worry."

"And Grandma—can I ask you something else?"

"Fire away, question-boy."

"Do you know where Rosaria is? Do you have her phone number?"

Grandma puffs out her lips, letting a rush of air escape. "We are always trying to track her down. Then she moves!" She lifts her chin. "But she always knows where *we* are."

"So, do you think that maybe some day—"

"Ack, my life is full of maybe-somedays! But I tell you a secret—you can keep a secret?"

Leo sits up in bed. "Yes."

"You're not to tell anybody, okay?"

"Okay."

"Your auntie Carmella's friend Lucy has a brother whose wife says she saw Rosaria—yes, it's true—she saw her a few months ago, and Rosaria has a child! Is true! And Carmella's friend Lucy's brother's wife told Rosaria that she should let that child meet his grandparents! Is true!" Grandma's cheeks are flushed.

"So, do you think—"

Grandma examines her nails. "Rosaria does not like to be told what to do, that's for sure."

"But at least there's hope, Grandma, right? At least there's hope."

Grandma Navy pats Leo's cheek. "Yes," she says, "as long as there are children, there is hope." She kisses his forehead. "Night-night, Giorgio."

Leo lets her mistake hover in the air over his bed.

In the morning, Leo can hear Grandma and

Grandpa downstairs in the kitchen, and he smells pancakes. He goes down the hall, past Carlo and Paolo's old room, to the one Contento is sleeping in. On the door is a hand-painted sign, trimmed with red and yellow flowers: *Angela and Maddalena*. Leo studies the door across from it, assuming that must have been Carmella and Rosaria's room, but there is no sign on the door. Leo turns the knob. Locked.

The Old Crone

Leo imagines what the old crone might have been like when she was young. Maybe she was always a little pinched, a little suspicious, or maybe she was something else entirely. Maybe she was a happy girl, like Rosaria was, and maybe something happened—or maybe many things happened—to make her shrivel up and become the old crone.

During a rehearsal break:

OLD CRONE: I wish that when Mr. Beeber wrote this play he'd put in more about the old crone when she was young, that he had told us her whole story.

LUCIA: What? That's ridiculous. Who cares about the old crone?

DONKEY: I wish Beeber had told us more about

	the donkey. Like how did the donkey learn to talk?
LUCIA:	Are you *joking*? If we should know more about anyone in this play, it's Lucia and her brother. I mean, what happened to their parents? How come we never know *that*?

In the play, the old crone and the villagers are suspicious of Rumpopo and the children. They don't trust anything that is new or different. By the end of the play, though, the old crone has heard Rumpopo's stories and seen the plays, and she seems changed by them, for the better.

But still, Leo thinks, there is a lot that is unexplained in this play. Maybe you can't tell it all in a play, or it would take days to perform, or weeks, or months. Maybe when you write a play you can only choose one very small part of one or two lives, but how do you choose which part, which lives? And maybe, even if you know someone really well—or think you do—you can never really know everything about them.

Leo is glad that the old crone seems happier by the end. She also gets the last line of the play, which makes Leo wonder if she is more important in the play than he had first thought. She is kind of like Rumpopo, who is old and grouchy at the beginning, but who is changed by the children and the stories.

Ruby says, "Maybe Rumpopo and the old crone should get married."

"You're kidding, right?" Leo says.

"No. I'm not. Think about it. They're both old and alone. They both like plays—"

"Huh."

>==<

Leo, the writer, is huddled in an attic garret in Paris. Cold air streams through cracks in the walls and roof. He is bent over a small table, writing feverishly by the light of a single candle rapidly burning its way to its molten end. Beside him, on the desk, is a stack of finished pages. On the floor are mounds of crumpled papers, the castoffs from earlier drafts. At last, he writes *The curtain closes. The end.*

He stacks the completed pages and turns to the beginning of *The Old Crone's Porch.*

Worries

Home almost-alone. Besides Leo, only Pietro is there, in his room playing his music full blast. Papa's still at work, Contento is at a friend's, and Mom has taken Nunzio to the doctor for a checkup.

Nunzio is much better. They are spoiling him rotten, so relieved that he seems his same old self, except for a reddened scar on his forehead. But sometimes at night, Leo wakes, anxious, and has to look into everyone's room to see if they are safe, and especially he has to kneel by Nunzio's bed to be sure he is breathing. Leo has a thousand new fears that something unexpected will happen, something bad, and he'd better stay alert.

Leo has been thinking a lot about Rosaria. How could Grandma and Grandpa Navy and Papa and all his brothers and sisters bear it when Rosaria left, and now, when they don't see her or hear from her? How often do they think about her? Why haven't they talked about her? Is it too painful? Is that why Ruby doesn't like to talk about her brother?

And Rumpopo, in the play. Leo knows it is just a play, but he often thinks about Rumpopo and his sister. She, too, leaves. Rumpopo's sister just grows up and moves away, and it's as if when she goes, she takes part of Rumpopo with her. He doesn't find that part again until the children come, when he tells them stories about himself and his sister.

Maybe Ruby would feel better if she told stories about her brother. Maybe Papa and Grandma and Grandpa would feel better if they told stories about Rosaria.

Another thing on Leo's mind: two important play rehearsals coming up and then the play, the real play. Up until now, it seemed they had so much time, and there was so much hopeful possibility—that their play would be perfect, that Leo would not utter a *glurt*—but now, such a short time to make it right, and a thousand things could go wrong, and what if it is a disaster? And only one night—one—for the real play. How can that be? All this time of preparation for only one night? And then it will be over?

And another thing stirring up Leo's brain: he has just finished reading his father's *Autobiography, Age of Thirteen*. It ends like this:

> *That is my life so far. Who knows what the future will bring?*

Beneath these words is a black-and-white photograph of Leo's father standing on his porch, a huge smile on his face, and his arms spread, as if he is welcoming whatever might come along. Leo stares at the photo a long time, looking for himself in his father, and then he closes the book. Leo opens the book again to the beginning and to the photo of Papa's whole family, including Rosaria, seated on the blanket. Close the book. Open the book. Close it. Open it. Each time, Rosaria is still there, and Leo's father is still standing there at the end, welcoming his future.

Leo remembers the photo of Ruby and her brother, Johnny. In the photo, they will always be hugging each other.

Leo takes the book up to the attic and returns it to the box of his father's things. He puts on the tap shoes, and off he goes, tapping like crazy, leaping over boxes, sliding and tapping, as if he could keep his whole life spinning safely there in the attic.

Rehearsals

The final two rehearsals are crucial, Mr. Beeber says. "These are your last chances to get it right before the final night." He knows the cast is nervous, so maybe that is why he makes the first rehearsal special.

MR. BEEBER: It will be a banana rehearsal.

DONKEY: A what?

MR. BEEBER: A banana rehearsal. Here is how it works: each character will substitute the word *banana* for one of his "real" words.

LUCIA: *Banana?* Did I hear you correctly?

MR. BEEBER: Yes, you did.

DONKEY: Every character does that? Even the donkey?

MR. BEEBER: Yes, even the donkey.

OLD CRONE:	And that's it? All we have to re-member is to use the word *banana* once?
MR. BEEBER:	Yes.
LUCIA:	Excuse me, Mr. Beeber, but exactly *why* are we doing this?
MR. BEEBER:	To keep you on your toes, to force you to concentrate and to stay in character. One stipulation, though: you must *not laugh*. This will not be as easy as you might think.

Already Leo is laughing, merely contemplating all those *bananas* flying around. He can't wait to do this rehearsal. He begins plotting exactly when he will slip in the word, imagining who he might trip up and how he might make someone else laugh.

And so they have the banana rehearsal. Mr. Beeber is right: it is not nearly as easy as it might sound. It is hard not to laugh and not to forget your lines when you hear the word *banana* instead of the word you expected.

Some highlights of the rehearsal:

RUMPOPO:	I am going to the porch now.
LUCIA:	Will you tell us about the green banana again?

And:

VILLAGER ONE:	We need to find out more about this old banana.

And:

DONKEY:	Trust me. Follow banana.

Leo saves the use of his *banana* until the very end of the play, to the last line, the last word, and at the end finally they all *can* laugh, and they laugh hard and long, remembering all those *bananas* and the odd expressions on people's faces when they were surprised by the *bananas*. It is a brilliant rehearsal.

The next day: the final rehearsal, a dress rehearsal. "No bananas allowed," Mr. Beeber cautions. "Complete and total seriousness. Everyone in costume, everyone stays in character. You *must* feel as if this is the *real* play."

They all wish it will go smoothly, but it does not. Everyone makes at least one error, and some people bumble all over the place, and it all feels clunky and rough and stale. At the end, several people are sobbing, Ruby-the-donkey has broken out in a rash from her costume, the girl who has played the rear end of the donkey faints because she has not been able to breathe, the dog pees on the donkey, and one of the villagers throws up on Rumpopo's porch.

When it is all over:

LUCIA: Mr. Beeber, you have got to post-
             pone the play!
MR. BEEBER: No-can-do.
LUCIA: But you *must*! This is too terribly
             awful.

Leo expects Mr. Beeber to pull out both his collar and his hair, but surprisingly, he remains extremely calm. He is even smiling.

MR. BEEBER: Cast, the show must go on, and go on it will! See you tomorrow evening! You will be fine, fine, fine.

LUCIA: But—

DONKEY: But—

OLD CRONE: But—

Jitters

Saturday. The play is tonight. Leo feels sick, as if he might die. Should he phone Mr. Beeber and tell him to find another old crone?

His family is no help. They expect Leo to do his chores, as usual. They do not understand the extreme agony he is feeling. He will probably have a heart attack, and then they will be sorry they made him clean the toilet on the day of the play.

At noon, Pietro calls, "Sardine! Fog boy!"

Leo is curled in his bed, a pillow over his head. "Leave me alone. I'm sick. I may be dying."

"Someone's at the door for you."

"Yeah, right."

"Seriously."

"You should not joke with a maybe-dying person."

Pietro throws his own pillow at Leo. "Ser-i-ous-ly. Someone's at the door for you. A *girl*."

Leo sits up. "Who?"

"Well, not a girl exactly—"

"Then what *exactly*?"

"She says to tell you it's the donkey."

Ruby is standing on the porch. She looks awful. Hair all messed up. Pale. Red rash on her arms. "Leo!"

"Ruby?"

"I can't do it."

"The play?"

Ruby clutches her stomach. "I'm sick."

Leo pats his own stomach. "Me, too."

Ruby leans toward Leo, staring into his eyes. "No—you don't *look* sick."

"Well, I *feel* sick."

"Me, too."

"You said that already. You can't be sick. Who's going to play the donkey?"

"Maybe we don't need the donkey."

"We *need* the donkey, Ruby."

They sit on the porch. Leo looks up and down the street. People are carrying on as usual, cars going in and out of driveways, kids playing in their yards.

"Maybe we're just nervous," Leo suggests.

"You think?"

"Yeah. Maybe it'll all be fine, just like Mr. Beeber says."

"You think?"

"Yeah."

Ruby sits there, wringing her hands. "Leo? You want to hear about my brother?"

"What? Now?"

"Well, if you don't want to—"

"No, no, I want to, but are you sure you feel up to it? I mean, you said you were feeling so sick and all—"

Ruby leans against Leo. "He was only four. He had the flu. We'd all had it—my mom and dad and me—but we got better. Johnny just got sicker and sicker, and one night he couldn't breathe, and his temperature went up to a hundred and five, and we took him to the emergency room—"

Leo takes Ruby's hand. She lets it rest there in his own.

"—and they admitted him, and my father took

me home while my mother stayed with him, and in the middle of the night we get this call—"

"From your mom?"

"From my mom. He died, Leo, just like that. He *died*. He never got better. He never came home."

"Come on, let's go for a walk. It's okay, come on." Leo is quiet until they turn toward Ruby's house. "I wish that hadn't happened, Ruby. I wish your brother was still here."

Ruby sniffles. "Me, too."

As they turn the next corner, Ruby says, "Hey, you know what I just remembered? Johnny had this one book that he wanted me to read to him, over and over and over. I must've read it a million times. *Green Eggs and Ham.*"

"Oh yeah," Leo says. "I bet I read that to Nunzio a million times, too."

"I wonder why I remembered that right now. Johnny kept telling my mom that he wanted green eggs and ham for breakfast—"

"Eww—"

"And he insisted and insisted. It was driving us crazy. So one day Mom gets some green food coloring and adds it to the eggs and ham—I mean it was truly disgusting looking—it looked like the eggs and ham were moldy—but Johnny was so excited."

"He ate them?"

"Yes! And all day long he went around saying, 'I *like* green eggs and ham. I do so like them, Ruby-I-am!'"

"Huh."

"Funny, the things you remember."

"Yeah."

The Play

It is beginning to snow as the family piles in the car to go to the play.

LEO: Hurry up! I'm going to be late. Mr. Beeber is going to kill me.

MOM: Contento! Pietro! Nunzio! Hurry!

NUNZIO: My thoothe—

PAPA: I am going to glue those shoes to your feet.

At school, Leo dashes past Grandma and Grandpa Navy ("They don't reserve seats for grandparents?") and some of the aunties, uncles, and cousins, and Leo is wishing none of them had come, what a horrible idea to invite them, because now they will all see what a terrible actor he is, and they will never let him forget it. Leo tears down the hallway and backstage, where Mr. Beeber is ready to *kill* him.

Leo scrambles into his costume, and everything is noise and confusion, and everyone is excited and nervous, and Mr. Beeber keeps telling them to be quiet, that the audience will hear them, and Lucia/Melanie is pacing back and forth, moaning:

LUCIA: I forgot my lines! What's my first line? Help me, somebody help me. Old crone, what's my first line?

OLD CRONE: I have no idea. What's *my* first line?

RUMPOPO: Where's my wig?

DONKEY: Where's my back end?

Leo peers around the curtain. Terrible thing to do! So many people! Hundreds of people, filling all the rows. He sees his papa with the rest of the family midway down the right side. He will definitely not look *there* when the play starts. It will make him too nervous. *What is my first line? When do I enter? What if I glurt?*

And then there is music, and they take their

places, and the lights come up, and the curtain opens, and the play—the real play!—begins. There is no time to think of other things. They are in the play, and the play moves forward, and there is Rumpopo standing on his porch, and there are Lucia and her brother and the little dog, and the dog is behaving very well, and the audience is silent, and then they laugh (when they are supposed to laugh)! It's as if all the characters become more aware and more alive, hearing that audience, as if they needed to hear them. Leo is astounded by the audience. He is in love with the audience.

Leo's turn. He is with the villagers. He says, "Ah, the wicked children," and the audience laughs, and Leo is surprised, because he did not know his line was funny, and he has to restrain himself from thanking the audience for their wonderful laughter. They zoom along, and halfway through the play, they are giddy backstage.

DONKEY: They like it! The audience likes the play!
LUCIA: They *love* the play!

RUMPOPO: And we're doing *great*! No one is messing up!

It is an incredible feeling, but they should not have congratulated themselves so soon. The next scene goes terribly. Lucia misses a line, her brother gets confused and tries to help her, and then it is all messy, and the audience is puzzled. They probably do not know whether to laugh or be embarrassed for the actors.

And then the donkey and Leo enter, and the donkey's back end trips, and the audience laughs, and the Ruby part of the donkey is mad, and she misses her line, and Leo tries to help, but he goofs and jumps to the next scene. It looks hopeless, and Leo is praying that Mr. Beeber will rescue them and let them begin again, but he does not rescue them. Instead, one of the villagers rescues them by whispering Leo's line to him, and the back end of the donkey gets herself together, and then the play moves on again, more smoothly, but they are all jittery now.

When Rumpopo and the children are doing

one of their magical scenes, the one where the feather becomes an emerald table, Leo steals a glance at the audience. They are entranced; they love the emerald table.

Leo dares to look for his family. They are caught up in the play, all of them leaning forward, watching. And then Leo sees that Papa and Grandma and Grandpa Navy are gripping one another's hands, staring intently at the stage. Leo wonders if Rumpopo's sister reminds them of Rosaria, and he is afraid that it will be too much for Grandma, and that she will rush from the room, unable to bear it. But then he has to turn away from his family, because the donkey is talking to him, and it is Leo's turn, and he is swallowed up in the play again. He does not have a chance to check on Grandma Navy until the very end of the scene.

She is sitting very straight in her chair, and both her hands are pressed to her mouth, but she does not look sad, as Leo expected. She looks as if she is seeing something miraculous, something amazing and puzzling and intriguing.

On they zoom to the end, and the actors finally

get into their stride, and they do not make mistakes, and just when they are at their very best, Leo feels the play rushing to its close, and before he knows it, they are all gathered on Rumpopo's porch, and Rumpopo speaks:

RUMPOPO: Thank you, one and all. I feel like a young lad again!

And Leo can hardly stand it, that the play is almost over. He says his line, the last line:

OLD CRONE: Maybe tomorrow you will all come to *my banan*—no! No! I mean *porch*! Maybe tomorrow you will all come to my *porch*?

Leo is so mortified that he almost *glurted* out that terrible *banana*, that something comes over him, and instead of simply standing there until the lights go down, as they have rehearsed, Leo ends by leaping off the porch and throwing his arms wide, and doing a little tap dance, a very little one, just a few short steps, which don't sound like tapping because there are no taps on his shoes.

The lights dim, the curtain closes, and Leo sees Mr. Beeber on the sidelines, giving him a puzzled look, but then he nods at Leo, as if he forgives him for his almost-banana and for his strange little dance. Then the curtain is opening again, and they are doing their bows, and the audience is clapping, and Leo sees his family applauding like mad, and he hears, amid all the other noise, "*Bravo, bravo, Leo!*" and he sees Papa and Mom and Grandma and Grandpa, and they are smiling, and they look proud.

When someone shouts "Author! Author!" Mr. Beeber blushes and steps forward. Melanie hands him a bouquet of flowers. Mr. Beeber bows and gestures toward the cast, and again the audience erupts in applause and cheers.

Leo does not want to leave the stage. He wants the audience to keep applauding and his family to keep shouting *"Bravo!"* and Papa and Mom and Grandma and Grandpa to keep smiling.

The News

In the lobby afterward, Leo's family swarms around him. "*Bravo*, Leo, *bravo!*" His papa ruffles his hair; his mom kisses him. Even cousin Tina says, "Cool. It was cool. My favorite part was the golden palace and the talking donkey. You were good, too."

Pietro punches Leo softly in the arm. "Yeah, you were good."

Nunzio wraps his arms around Leo. "You were the betht! The betht one!"

Contento hands him a card, which she has decorated with red flowers. The envelope says FOR MY BROTHER, THE ACTOR. "Cool old crone," she says.

Grandma and Grandpa Navy are beaming. "It was *molto* good!" Grandma Navy says, and Grandpa nods in agreement. Grandma leans toward Leo and whispers in his ear. "I have some news for you."

Leo sees Ruby standing with her parents. "Just a minute, Grandma," he says, and he goes to Ruby. "You okay?"

She smiles, but her eyes are brimming, as if she will burst into tears. "I'm fine," she says. "It was fun."

"Want to come over tomorrow? I mean, my house is kind of crazy, but—"

"Sure, Leo. I'll come." She places her arm on his sleeve. "Thanks."

When Leo returns to his family, Grandma pulls him aside. "I'm telling you first. Well, Grandpa knows, and your papa knows, and Carmella, but I'm telling you first before all the others."

There is commotion all around as families call to one another and search for coats and begin to stream out of the building. Leo strains to hear his grandma. And suddenly he knows what she is going to say. "Rosaria?" he says. "Is it about Rosaria?"

"Yes!" Grandma beams. "You know I told you about Carmella's friend's brother's wife seeing Rosaria and about the child—"

"Yes, yes, and—?"

"Well, you know after we were looking at those pictures? And you were asking about her? Well, I had to do something. So I called Carmella, who called her friend, who called her brother—"

"Grandma! What happened?"

"I get the phone number. Of Rosaria. The new phone number. I call. I get an answering machine! You imagine? An answering machine! Not even with her voice, with some man's voice—"

"Grandma! Did you leave a message?"

"Well, no—"

"No? You didn't leave a message? Grandma—"

"Not the first time. But then I called back and I told the answering machine who I was—I said I was an old grandma who wanted to see her Rosaria and her child—my grandchild. That's what I said. I said I have a lot of grandchildren, but you can never have too many grandchildren, and that child needs to know his grandma. That's what I said."

"And? Did she call back?"

"What? Oh. No. Not yet." Grandma's hands flutter in the air. "But I left that message. Maybe she will answer it?"

Leo glances toward the door as Ruby and her parents leave. He wishes Ruby could leave a message for her brother.

When Leo turns and sees Papa at his side, he wonders if Papa will ever talk to Rosaria, if he will ever see her again. How happy Papa would be to see her!

Papa clears his throat and leans down, looking Leo in the eye. "You were good," Papa says, "really good."

For Leo, this is like hearing he's won ten Nobel Prizes, and he wants to say something, but the words are all jumbled in his head.

His papa pats his shoulder. "You know, I used to do plays—with—with—with Rosaria."

Leo nods. He feels as if his father has given him a golden nugget. He touches his papa's arm. "That's cool, Papa."

And then there is a rush of people waving and streaming out the door, and Leo's family piles in the car. Nunzio leans his head on Leo's shoulder and whispers, "You didn't even glurt!"

Finale: What We Did Today

It is Sunday, and already everyone is rushing around because the relatives are coming. Leo is groggy. Last night after the play, as he lay in bed, his mind was swirling with images of Ruby and Johnny, and of his grandma's hands fluttering in the air over Rosaria, and his papa smiling, and the audience's laughter, and his family shouting *"Bravo!"* He replayed *Rumpopo's Porch* in his mind, from start to finish, going through everyone's lines, remembering how it happened in the real play, and then changing the goofs so that it played perfectly.

In his dreams, he was in the play again, but everyone was all jumbled up. Papa was playing the part of Rumpopo, and Rosaria was there, too, with her little white dog. At the end of the play, his papa said, "Thank you. I feel like a young lad again," and hundreds of emeralds rained down from the sky.

This morning, at breakfast, Pietro says to Nunzio, "You know, the donkey came to see the old crone yesterday."

Nunzio stops, midbite, and says, "Really? The donkey? From the play?"

"Yep," says Pietro. "That's the one."

"She's coming over today, too," Leo says.

Contento holds her fork like a microphone. "Announcement. Announcement, please. The old crone has an admirer."

"Huh," Leo says. He turns to Papa. He wants to say something about Rosaria, but before he can form the words, his mom says, "Aye yie yie! Sardine-o, come wash this pan. Contento, iron that tablecloth. Nunzio, where are your shoes?"

At the sink, Leo imagines a story: *Leonardo's Porch*. A boy, Leo, will be standing there at the beginning—but while Leo is imagining this, he is again interrupted, this time by Papa. "Leo? Can you come with me a minute?"

Leo figures Papa wants him to do another chore, so he finishes washing the pan and follows him, grumbling in his head about the writer being interrupted in the middle of Great Ideas. When Papa starts up the attic stairs, Leo worries that Papa has found out that Leo has been in his things and tapping in his shoes and reading his *Autobiography, Age of Thirteen,* and Leo is afraid that Papa will be extremely angry.

Sure enough, Papa searches through the boxes and locates the one with his things in it. Papa rummages through the box, finds the tap shoes, and hands them to Leo.

PAPA: Would you like these?

LEO: What? Me? But I thought—they're yours—

PAPA: It's okay. You have them.

Leo puts on the shoes as Papa continues to rummage through the box.

PAPA: Leo? I don't know if this would interest you—

Papa stands there, holding the blue book, *Autobiography, Age of Thirteen*, in his hands.

LEO: But if it's yours—
PAPA: It's a little book I wrote when I was about your age. You like stories. It might interest you. Maybe not . . .

Leo takes the book from him. He feels honored that his father trusts him with his book, but he also feels bad that he can't tell Papa the truth, that he has already read it.

Papa is about to close the box when he sees something and digs to the bottom. He retrieves a straggly red bear, stares at it, and then presses it to his chest. "Chili Bear," he says. "It was Rosaria's." He carries it with him as he starts down the steps. "Well," he adds, "I'd better go fix that toilet. . . ."

Leo wants to call him back and thank him, and he wants to ask how he felt when Rosaria left and how he feels now, and he wants to ask him about all those long-ago dreams and goals, and a million things Leo wants to ask him, but instead he starts tapping. He can't help it, off he goes, feeling so full of his family and the play, as if he is standing on the porch of his life, like his father stands in that last photo in his book.

At the foot of the stairs he hears:

PIETRO: What's that racket up there?

PAPA: *Zitti!* It's Leo. Leave him alone. He's just trying to grow up.

The Curtain Closes . . .

If you want to read or perform the play . . .

RUMPOPO'S PORCH

by Bill Beeber

THE CAST

Rumpopo, an old man
Lucia, a young girl
Pahchay, a young boy
Lucia and Pahchay's Dog
Young Rumpopo (played by Pahchay)
Sola, Rumpopo's sister (played by Lucia)
Wonder, Rumpopo and Sola's dog
(played by Lucia and Pahchay's Dog)
Villagers
Old Crone
Donkey

Scene 1

At center stage is the exterior of a tumbledown cabin with a porch. Trees surrounding, one of which is hollow. As the curtain opens, old Rumpopo *is standing on the porch, facing audience, talking to himself.*

Rumpopo: Aye, my bones ache. My life is empty. It is over. What use is there for an old man like me?

(*Enter the children,* Lucia *and* Pahchay, *and their dog. They look worn and bedraggled.*)

Rumpopo: Who's there? What do you want?

Lucia: Pardon, kind sir, but we are two abandoned children who have traveled long and far, and we have lost our way. May we rest here a moment?

Rumpopo: I'm an old man. There's nothing here for you.

Pahchay:	Pardon, kind sir, but do you have a cup of water to spare?
Rumpopo:	(*grumbling*) Water? Oh, I suppose. There's a well—over there.
Lucia:	I'll fetch some. Shall I bring some for you, kind sir?
Rumpopo:	(*shrugs*) If you can manage.

(Lucia *and dog go to well.* Pahchay *follows, picking up pieces of wood as he goes.*)

Rumpopo:	(*to self*) Children! Abandoned! And a dog! I am too old for this.
Lucia:	Have you a cup, kind sir?
Rumpopo:	Over here—on the railing.
Lucia:	Would you like some, kind sir?
Rumpopo:	Yes. (*hesitates*) But you go first. You look thirsty.
Lucia:	Thank you, kind sir.
Pahchay:	I've brought you some wood for your fire. What fine wood there is here. Would you like me to stack it for you, kind sir?

Rumpopo:	Erm, yes, thank you. (*hesitates*) You don't need to keep calling me "kind sir." My name is Rumpopo.
Lucia:	Rumpopo! What a beautiful name, kind sir! I am Lucia, and this is my brother, Pahchay.
Rumpopo:	And you say you are abandoned? And have traveled long and far? And are lost?
Lucia:	Aye, kind—Rumpopo, sir.
Rumpopo:	Your parents? Where are they?
Lucia:	No idea, kind Rumpopo sir.
Rumpopo:	Just Rumpopo. Not "kind," not "sir," if you please.
Lucia:	Aye, ki—Rumpopo.
Pahchay:	We have been alone for some time, Rumpopo.
Rumpopo:	Alone? All alone?
Lucia:	Except for our dog, of course.
Rumpopo:	It seems a friendly little dog.
Pahchay:	Oh, he is, Rumpopo sir—
Rumpopo:	No "sir."
Pahchay:	Yes, Rumpopo. Our dog has kept us

	safe on many a long and dark night.
Rumpopo:	And where will you go from here?
Lucia:	We've no idea, Rumpopo. Perhaps you'd be so kind as to show us the way to a sheltered spot where we might sleep tonight? Are these woods safe, would you say?
Rumpopo:	(*troubled*) One never knows for sure. My porch might be safer for you.
Lucia:	Oh, Rumpopo! Truly? We could sleep here on your porch?
Rumpopo:	I suppose you could stay the night. Just one night.
Lucia:	Oh, we thank you, kind and noble sir!
Pahchay:	Thank you, most kind and noble Rumpopo, sir!

Scene 2

The village well. As the scene opens, the villagers and the old crone are gathered stage left, around the well. Some are filling buckets; others are gathered around to join in the gossip. Rumpopo, Lucia, Pahchay, *and dog are seen leaving the village stage right.*

Villager One:	Who is that old man?
Villager Two:	Where's he from?
Villager Three:	I heard those children call him something—
Villager Four:	—Rimpo?
Villager Five:	—Rompo?
Villager Six:	—Rappapo?
Old Crone:	Rumpopo.
Villager One:	What's he up to?
Villager Two:	Aye, what?
Villager Three:	I do not trust him.
Villager Four:	Nor I!
Villager Five:	And who are those children?

Villager Six:	Aye! Appearing out of nowhere!
Old Crone:	Ah, yes, the wicked children.
Villager One:	Wicked?
Old Crone:	Surely.
Villager Six:	Appearing out of nowhere!
Villager Three:	I do not trust them.
Villager Four:	Nor I!
Villager Two:	They want something!
Villager Five:	Wicked!

The cabin. Rumpopo, *the children, and dog enter from stage left.* Lucia *is skipping ahead;* Pahchay *is holding* Rumpopo's *hand.*

Rumpopo: I am going to the porch now.

Lucia: Will you tell us about the green woods again?

Rumpopo: Aye, Lucia, that I will do, most happily.

Pahchay: And the young Rumpopo? Will you tell us about him?

Rumpopo: Aye.

Pahchay: And your little sister, Sola, too? And the dog?

Rumpopo: (*sitting on porch*) Aye, Pahchay, aye.

(*As* Rumpopo *begins his story, the lights dim, soft music plays, and* Pahchay *and* Lucia *step forward to act the parts of* Young Rumpopo *and his sister,* Sola.)

Rumpopo:	When I was a young lad and the apple trees were in blossom . . .

(Young Rumpopo *and his sister,* Sola, *are gathered around a box on the porch steps.*)

Sola:	Oh, Rumpopo! A puppy!
Young Rumpopo:	Aye, Sola! For us!
Sola:	What shall we name him?
Young Rumpopo:	He must have a special name.
Sola:	For he is a special dog, isn't he, Rumpopo?
Young Rumpopo:	Aye. I think we should call him—Wonder!
Sola:	Wonder? Yes, Wonder!
Young Rumpopo:	And he will lead us to wonderful things—
Sola:	Magical things!
Young Rumpopo:	Amazing—
Sola:	—and spectacular—
Young Rumpopo:	—and exciting things!

Scene 4

The village well, as before.

Villager One:	We need to find out more about this old Rimpo—Rompo—Rumpopo and the children.
Villager Two:	Yes, but how?
Old Crone:	I am getting an idea.
Villager Three:	I do not trust that old Rimpo—Rompo—Rumpopo!
Villager Four:	Or those children!
Old Crone:	I'll find his cabin.
Villager Five:	You will?
Old Crone:	I will go there—
Villager Six:	Be careful!
Villager One:	It might be dangerous—
Villager Two:	—perilous—
Old Crone:	(*not so sure now*) Um.
Villager Three:	—nasty—
Villager Four:	—hazardous—

Old Crone:	(*even less sure*) Um. Well—
Villager Five:	—treacherous—
Villager Six:	—risky!
Villager One:	Be careful!
Old Crone:	(*worried*) Ummmm. Okay. I *guess.*

Scene 5

The forest.

Old Crone: (*to self*) I will find out what that old
              Rumpopo is up to. I hope this is not
              too—too—dangerous or risky or
              hazardous or—

(*Enter* Donkey.)

Donkey: Perhaps I can help you.
Old Crone: You? A donkey?
Donkey: Not just any donkey. I can lead you
              to Rumpopo's and show you where
              to hide, the better to listen.
Old Crone: I don't know—
Donkey: Trust me. Follow me.
Old Crone: I've never followed a donkey before.
Donkey: No?

Old Crone:	Never. Is this, um, treacherous? Hazardous?
Donkey:	Depends.
Old Crone:	On what?
Donkey:	On whether we encounter snakes or bees or tigers or—
Old Crone:	Wait. Are there snakes and bees and tigers around here?
Donkey:	No. Not usually. But you never know, do you?
Old Crone:	(*worried*) Ummmm.
Donkey:	Trust me. Follow me.
Old Crone:	(*worried*) Ummmm. Well. *Okay.*

Scene 6

Rumpopo's cabin. Rumpopo, *the children, and dog are on the porch.* Donkey, *followed by* Old Crone, *enter at stage left, behind trees.*

Donkey:	(*to old crone*) This is an opportune place to hide yourself.
Old Crone:	Where?
Donkey:	Here, in this hollow tree.
Old Crone:	(*examining tree*) There aren't any bees or snakes in here, are there? Or tigers?
Donkey:	Shh, just get in.

(Old Crone *slips into tree;* Donkey *remains nearby.*)

Lucia:	More, Rumpopo? Please will you tell us about the emerald table again?
Rumpopo:	Aye, Lucia. In the forest, we found—

(*As* Rumpopo *talks, lights dim, soft music plays, and* Lucia *and* Pahchay *step forward with dog, as before, to act the parts of* Young Rumpopo, Sola, *and* Wonder.)

Young Rumpopo:	Look, Sola! Wonder has found something—
Sola:	A feather!
Young Rumpopo:	What is it, Wonder? Is there something magical here?
Sola:	Such a beautiful emerald-green feather.
Young Rumpopo:	And perhaps, if we wave it in the air—
Sola:	And close our eyes—
Young Rumpopo:	—and wish—
Sola:	—and imagine—
Young Rumpopo:	—it shall become—

(*Lights come up on an emerald table, laden with food, at stage right.*)

Sola:	An emerald table! (*touching table*) So green, so beautiful!
Young Rumpopo:	(*touching plates*) With golden plates—so sparkling!
Sola:	And food—
Young Rumpopo:	—so delicious—
Sola:	So *very* delicious!
Young Rumpopo:	Fit for kings and queens!
Sola:	And we will bring Mother and Father—
Young Rumpopo:	And we will dine until our stomachs burst!
Old Crone:	(*in tree*) What? How did they do that? What magic is at work here?
Donkey:	You can see the emerald table?
Old Crone:	Of course! It's right there—

The village well, as before.

Villager One:	Well? What did you find out?
Old Crone:	The children seem to live there, with Rumpopo.
Villager Two:	Perhaps he has kidnapped them!
Villager Three:	I told you he was strange.
Old Crone:	And they do some sort of magic—
Villager Four:	What? Is it witchcraft?
Villager Five:	I told you! Did I not tell you?
Old Crone:	It doesn't seem like witchcraft—
Villager Six:	What is it they do?
Old Crone:	It is more like a play, I think.
Villager One:	A play?
Villager Two:	What is a play?
Villager Three:	Witchcraft!
Old Crone:	Do you remember when we were young? There was a play in the village, was there not?

Villager Four:	Never!
Villager Five:	Witchcraft!
Villager Six:	Wait, I do seem to recall—there *was* a play! There was an old man in it—
Villager One:	Rimpo—Rompo—Rumpopo?
Villager Six:	No, no, not Rumpopo. He wasn't an old man then. He would have been a boy.
Villager Two:	Wait, I remember. The play was about an old man and his daughter, and they lived on an island.
Villager Three:	Oh, yes! I remember!
Old Crone:	Yes, yes, and what Rumpopo and the children do is like a play. There was a feather, and it turned into an emerald table—
Villager One:	Witchcraft! It sounds rather dangerous—
Villager Two:	—rather perilous—
Old Crone:	(*worried*) Um.
Villager Three:	—rather nasty—

Villager Four:	—rather hazardous—
Old Crone:	(*more worried*) Um. Well—
Villager Five:	—rather treacherous—
Villager Six:	—rather risky!
Villager One:	Be careful!
Old Crone:	(*very worried*) Ummmm. *Ohhh-kay.*

Scene 8

Old Crone *is in the hollow tree with* Donkey *nearby.*
Rumpopo *and the children are on the porch.*

Donkey:	So, have you discovered any-thing of interest?
Old Crone:	Shh, listen—
Lucia:	Oh, Rumpopo, please will you tell us again about the rock?
Rumpopo:	Aye, aye, the rock—

(*Lights dim, soft music plays as* Lucia *and* Pahchay *and dog move forward, as before, to play the parts of* Young Rumpopo, Sola, *and* Wonder.)

Sola:	Rumpopo, look! Wonder has found something—
Young Rumpopo:	A rock!
Sola:	A *golden* rock—
Young Rumpopo:	Aye, Sola! Perhaps real gold?

Sola:	Most certainly.
Young Rumpopo:	And perhaps if we toss it high in the air—
Sola:	—and make a wish—
Young Rumpopo:	—and imagine—
Sola:	—and dream—
Young Rumpopo:	—it might become—

(Rumpopo *tosses the rock high into the air, and as he does so, there is a burst of light, revealing at far right a golden palace.*)

Sola:	A palace!
Young Rumpopo:	A grand palace, a golden palace!

(*They touch the walls, the windows.*)

Sola:	So magnificent!
Young Rumpopo:	So luxurious!
Sola:	And we will bring Mother and Father here, and we will all live here together—

Young Rumpopo:	—forever—
Sola:	—and ever!
Young Rumpopo:	Like kings and queens—
Sola:	—and princes and princesses!
Old Crone:	(*in tree*) Oh! A palace!
Donkey:	You can see the palace?
Old Crone:	Of course I can. A golden palace! How do they *do* that?

Scene 9

The village well, as before.

Villager One:	A palace?
Old Crone:	A *golden* palace.
Villager Two:	From a *rock*?
Villager Three:	Impossible! Witchcraft!
Villager Four:	It sounds terribly hazardous—
Villager Five:	—terribly treacherous—
Old Crone:	I do wish you'd stop saying that—
Villager Six:	But was it real? The palace?
Old Crone:	I saw it before my very eyes.
Villager One:	A palace?
Old Crone:	A *golden* palace.
Villager Two:	Impossible!
Villager Three:	—and terribly nasty—
Villager Four:	—terribly hazardous—
Old Crone:	Ack!

Scene 10

The cabin, with Old Crone *in tree and* Donkey *nearby. The lights are already dim, but there is no music playing.* Old Rumpopo *is alone on the porch.*

Old Rumpopo: Sola? Wonder? Where are you?
Old Crone: (*to Donkey*) Where are they?
Donkey: Shh, watch.
Old Rumpopo: Sola! Wonder! Sola! Sola! Sola!

(*All is silent.*)

Old Crone: Where'd they go?

(*Stage goes dark.*)

Scene 11

The cabin porch. Old Rumpopo *sits in chair, head in hands.* Lucia, Pahchay, *and their dog are at his feet.*

Lucia: Oh, Rumpopo, where did they go?

Pahchay: Were they killed?

Rumpopo: No, no. They were not killed. Sola grew up. She went away.

Pahchay: And Wonder?

Rumpopo: Wonder went with Sola.

Lucia: And did you never see them again?

Rumpopo: A few times. Not enough.

Old Crone: (*in tree*) Poor Rumpopo!

Donkey: Perhaps. Perhaps not.

The village well, as before.

Villager Four:	A little girl—Sola? And a dog?
Villager Five:	Gone?
Villager Six:	But is it real? Did it really happen?
Villager One:	You said it was a play—
Villager Two:	So it wasn't real—
Old Crone:	It was a play, but—
Villager Three:	But what?
Old Crone:	But—but it was real.
Villager Five:	Poor Rumpopo. All alone.
Villager Six:	He never saw them again?
Old Crone:	A few times. Not enough.
Villager Three:	Not enough.
Villager Four:	And the young boy?
Old Crone:	That was Rumpopo.
Villager Two:	But he is old.
Old Crone:	Once, he was young.
Villager One:	It was real?

Old Crone:	It was real.
Villager Five:	And the emerald table?
Villager Six:	The golden palace?
Old Crone:	Real.
Villager One:	And not dangerous?
Villager Two:	Not perilous?
Villager Three:	Not nasty?
Old Crone:	No.
Villager Four:	Not hazardous?
Villager Five:	Not treacherous?
Villager Six:	Not risky?
Old Crone:	No.
Villager One:	And the table, the palace—?
Old Crone:	Real.
Villager Two:	Real?
Villager Three:	Real?
Old Crone:	Real.

Scene 13

The cabin. Rumpopo, Lucia, Pahchay, *and their dog are on porch.* Old Crone *is in hollow tree, with* Donkey *nearby.*

Old Crone:	Poor, poor Rumpopo. How will he go on?
Donkey:	Watch.
Rumpopo:	What story would you like to hear today?
Lucia:	Oh, Rumpopo, you do not have to tell us a story today.
Pahchay:	You are too sad.
Rumpopo:	I have been sad for too many years.

(*Lights dim, soft music plays, as* Lucia *and* Pahchay *and dog move forward, as before.*)

Young Rumpopo:	Look, Sola! Wonder has found something—

Sola:	A feather!
Young Rumpopo:	What is it, Wonder? Is there something magical here?
Sola:	Such a beautiful emerald-green feather.
Young Rumpopo:	And perhaps, if we wave it in the air—
Sola:	It shall become—

(*Lights come up again on the emerald table, laden as before, with food, at stage right.*)

Sola:	An emerald table!
Young Rumpopo:	With golden plates—
Sola:	And food—
Young Rumpopo:	For kings and queens!
Sola:	And we will bring Mother and Father—
Young Rumpopo:	And we will dine until our stomachs burst!
Old Crone:	(*in tree*) The emerald table! Again!
Donkey:	Yes.

Old Crone:	Just as before!
Donkey:	Yes.
Old Crone:	And look, there is Sola!
Donkey:	And Wonder.

(*Lights come up.* Lucia *and* Pahchay *return to porch.*)

Lucia:	Oh, I love the emerald table story, Rumpopo.
Pahchay:	And tomorrow, will you tell us again about the golden rock? The palace?
Rumpopo:	Aye. I will.

Scene 14

The cabin. All of the villagers, *who have brought food, are gathered on the porch with the* Old Crone, Rumpopo, Lucia, Pahchay, *and the dog. The* Donkey *lingers nearby.*

Rumpopo:	Thank you for these generous gifts. I am overwhelmed.
Old Crone:	(*handing him a blanket*) Here, this is for you. I made it.
Lucia:	How beautiful!
Villager One:	And I made the cake—
Pahchay:	Delicious!
Villager Two:	The roast is mine—
Rumpopo:	Thank you, thank you. What can I do to repay you?
Villager Three:	Will you tell us—
Villager Four:	—something amazing—
Villager Five:	—and spectacular—
Villager Six:	—and even, maybe, a little

	hazardous? Treacherous? Risky?
Villager One:	Will you tell us about the emerald table?
Villager Two:	And the golden rock?
Villager Three:	And the palace?
Rumpopo:	Aye, aye. That I can do. We will have emerald tables and golden palaces and maybe a little hazard, some treachery, some risk . . .
Villager Four:	Oh, thank you!
Rumpopo:	No, thank *you*, one and all. I feel like a young lad again!
Old Crone:	Maybe tomorrow you will all come to *my* porch?

The End

Literature Circle Questions

Use the questions and activities that follow to get more out of reading *Replay* by Sharon Creech.

1. In the midst of his busy, noisy family, Leo often imagines himself in completely different circumstances. What are some of Leo's fantasies? Describe at least five.

2. The last time Leo was in a school play, he left feeling embarrassed about his performance (p. 16). What happened to make Leo feel ashamed?

3. Leo discovers and reads his father's childhood journal *Autobiography, Age of Thirteen*. What interesting information does Leo learn about his father's childhood from reading the journal?

4. Who is Ruby, and what role does she play in Leo's life?

5. Leonardo's family often calls him *sardine* and *fog boy*. What do these nicknames reveal about Leo and his relationship with his family? How does Leo feel about his nicknames?

6. The first time that Leo's father sees his son wearing his old tap shoes, he angrily commands him to take the shoes off. His father yells, "Don't you go through my things. Those are *my* things, what little of my own that I have in this zoo-house" (p. 7). Why do you think Leo's father is so angry to see his son wearing the shoes?

7. Have you ever participated in a play, concert, or other performance for which you had to practice? Compare your experience in preparing for a performance to Leo's rehearsals with Mr. Beeber for *Rumpopo's Porch*.

8. As part of the rehearsals for *Rumpopo's Porch*, Mr. Beeber asks his students to do some strange assignments, such as writing about the childhoods of their characters (p. 28) or inserting the word "banana" into their lines (pp. 155–156). Why does Mr. Beeber ask his students to do these things? What might Mr. Beeber hope his students learn from their participation in the play?

9. In the chapter titled "Papa," Leo remembers what his father was like before he had a heart attack three years ago. Compare and contrast Leo's father before and after his heart attack. How has his father's attitude and relationship with his children changed?

10. Pietro, one of Leo's younger brothers, used to admire his big brother, but now Pietro is interested only in football (pp. 32–34). In your own words, explain how Pietro has changed since he was younger. How does Leo feel about the changes in his little brother?

11. How has the experience of being in the play *Rumpopo's Porch* changed the way Leo sees himself? Has being in the play changed Leo's life in any other ways? Give examples from the story.

12. Near the end of the novel, we learn that Leo's grandma, Navy, has left a phone message for her daughter Rosaria, after many years of not speaking. Imagine the scene when Rosaria returns to her family with her son after her long absence. How do her parents and siblings respond to her return? How does Leo feel about meeting his aunt Rosaria for the first time?

13. Parts of *Replay* are written in script form, complete with stage directions. Why do you think the author decided to write the story in this way?

14. As one of four children, Leo often feels overlooked in his family, and he tells his friend Ruby that he thinks it would be nice to be an only child. In your opinion, what is the ideal number of children in a family? Would you enjoy being in a large family like Leo's? What are the advantages and disadvantages of being an only child?

15. Leo imagines a scene in which every student in his class is given a Life Script to see what will happen in the future. If given the chance, would you want to learn about your future? Do you think it would make your life easier or harder to know what lies ahead for you?

Note: These Literature Circle questions are keyed to Bloom's Taxonomy *as follows: Knowledge: 1–3; Comprehension: 4–6; Application: 7; Analysis: 8–10; Synthesis: 11–12; Evaluation: 13–15.*

Activities

1. Leo spends a lot of time thinking about how his father, his brother Pietro, and his sister Contento have changed since they were very young. Interview someone who has known you for a very long time to find out how you have changed since you were a young child. From what you learned about yourself as a child, write a short scene from your life in the form of a play.

2. Leo reads his father's two lists of goals, one for high school and one for life. He then tries to write his own lists of goals and finds it harder than he imagined (pp. 86–90). What are your goals? Make two lists of goals, one titled "Middle School" and one titled "Life."

3. With a group of classmates, select a scene or two from *Rumpopo's Porch* to present in a readers' theater. Assign parts, and practice your readings out loud. Be prepared to share your readers' theater with your class.